THE FATAL ENTRANCE

A farmhouse in the Eastern Transvaal has been converted into a hostel for guests by its owner, Thalia du Mont. On holiday there is an assorted array of people, but most of them are not what they appear on the surface. It soon emerges that there is on the farm an unknown killer in pursuit of a legendary treasure, and a series of deaths results from this 'fatal entrance'. The horror of the situation is compounded when flood waters pour down the valley, isolating the farm . . .

ROBERT BARRATT

THE FATAL ENTRANCE

Complete and Unabridged

LINFORD
Leicester

First published in Great Britain in 1975 by
Robert Hale Limited
London

First Linford Edition
published 2005
by arrangement with
Robert Hale Limited
London

British Library CIP Data

Barratt, Robert
    The fatal entrance.—Large print ed.—
Linford mystery library
    1. Transvaal (South Africa)—Fiction
    2. Suspense fiction
    3. Large type books
    I. Title
    823.9'14 [F]

ISBN 1–84395–768–X

Published by
F. A. Thorpe (Publishing)
Anstey, Leicestershire

Set by Words & Graphics Ltd.
Anstey, Leicestershire
Printed and bound in Great Britain by
T. J. International Ltd., Padstow, Cornwall

This book is printed on acid-free paper

1

When it was all over I was, for some reason, often reminded of Lady Macbeth's words to her husband as she prepared to 'welcome' the king to Dunsinane:

> The raven himself is hoarse
> That croaks the fatal entrance of Duncan
> Under my battlements.

But this wasn't a castle. It was a rather ordinary farmhouse in fact. Though then again 'ordinary' wasn't quite the right word for a home as unpretentiously pleasing as the farm-house at 'Bloedplaas'. And how one begins looking at portents when one has been granted hindsight, because this was indeed to become a 'farm of blood'. And, yet again, the horrors of 'Bloedplas' would be off-set, even at their height, by the incredible beauty of the place.

It had stopped some years before being

a large-scale farm. The present owner kept on only a few hundred acres for a farm-house which no longer deserved the name, except in its lovely isolation. For 'Bloedplaas' had become a guest farm, an unusual, homely one, not the formidable 'Bushveld Perpendicular' of so many of these places with their assertive Coca-Cola freezers, and their commercialised curios.

The farm lay in the Eastern Transvaal lowveld, below the great dip of the escarpment. It was a territory of mimosas, Kaffirboom, intensely red poinsettias, wild creeper and lush greenery, on the edge of the timber world of Sabie and Graskop. Above it towered 'De Kaap' (which those old Trekkers had thought was the Cape of Good Hope reborn), high architectural mountains battening against an intensely blue sky. In the valley, too, were the old settlements of the first Transvaal gold-miners. At the ghost town of Pilgrim's Rest, at Barberton, at the legendary Eureka City, the earth bore the scars of their digging.

The farm itself was quite different from its surroundings in one notable way: the colour of its soil. Red, deep-red, and that is certainly where the name 'Farm of Blood' came from.

I had better also explain about myself. I am a journalist, Simon Digby, the author of a few successful books ('travel', I think, would be their generic description) about parts of South Africa, particularly the Transvaal and its Lowveld.

I had for a long time been a friend of Thalia du Mont, to whom the farm now belonged. I was glad when she gave up farming and began the guest farm. For how well she did it! Every now and again I like eating and drinking well, and on her farm this was more than possible. The house itself was, in its style, unique. It had been built on a simple principle: six white-washed rondawels of unbaked brick grouped around a porch of high dark thatch, which even in the fiercest heat of summer made a blue pool of coolness. A big living-room, like the stoep raftered by pine trunks, reached behind, its floors of grey, smooth cement partly covered by a big, faded, but still beautiful Persian rug, the faint red of its colour every now and again taking fire from some change of cloud outside, or, in winter, from the burning logs. The two outer rondawels to the side of the house were reached by crossing a small courtyard. But I won't go on to describe the house now. I'll try to let its quality, its atmosphere emerge as I go on telling my story. By the way, one important thing: the house has no electric lights.

At night the living-room, when in winter it is not simply left to the red glow of the flames, is dotted with gas and hurricane lamps, so that in the silence of the veld its own spirit becomes pervasive, and we are enclosed in a small brightly lit capsule. When the lights go off we are left to the lovely silence of the night, domed by a huge sky of stars. And I'd better also say this before I leave the matter of description. I've visited a great many notable houses in my line of business, particularly when inspecting the lives of the great for my magazine, or for one of my books. They have been thickly carpeted, richly curtained, with the most up-to-date Swedish or the oldest antique furniture, with paintings I could never aspire to; yet none of these houses has been more comely than that at Bloedplaas, with its walls of unbaked brick, and its floors of grey cement.

I was coming to spend two weeks at the guest house. I usually tried to choose a quiet time, but Thalia's own particular brand of hospitality was becoming well-known, and I had learnt that her hostelry (as she sometimes called it) would be full for most of my stay. I didn't have any other time at my disposal this year: I had finished my latest book, and was about to go on to the next. I'm not telling this story well, because I had better also explain that I was mildly middle-aged (a fairly youthful thirty-eight), unmarried, quiet, yet with a built-in love of texture, atmosphere, veld and sky.

I had left Johannesburg early because I liked to see the sun coming through that first gateway to Schoeman's Kloof. The gate to the lowveld we called it: here one would drop thousands of feet in a few minutes — from the rather barren yellow of the highveld, one would in moments sink into paradise. Whatever the season the lowveld was verdant. Aloes would come marching down the mountain-sides in armies, their red tips brilliant spears against the rank green. There would be creepers, Mimosas in incredible yellow profusion, red poinsettias, blue Jacarandas if the season was right. The place was alive with glitter. It was warm even in winter — very hot of course in summer — but the trees were high and arching, and the cool of their shade delicious. It was, I found, a marvellous place in which to eat hardboiled eggs (which I did when I travelled in the morning); or at midday, to drink red wine, or freezing beer, or gin and tonic. Food took on the aroma of its setting and everything seemed to be good.

Perhaps not this particular summer, for even beauty can be destroyed by the presence of a beast.

From Schoeman's Kloof I continued at an easy pace to Montrose Falls, where I stopped for a cup of coffee, and tranquilly watched the broad stream of the Crocodile River being spurred over the resisting stones. Then back into my Peugeot (which was purring contentedly) and on past the De Kaap mountains, past Nelspruit boiling in its late morning shimmer, along the White River road — and then turning between the thick roadside scrub, suddenly and dramatically I became part of the farm road spearing into the mountains. It was almost deeper than blood.

★ ★ ★

Leaving the red track I drove into the sudden twilightblue of Thalia's avenue. The trees closed over my head, and only glimpses of sun fell in dapples on the road. At evening this was the chosen abode of the wood owls. It was first with pleasure, and later with foreboding, that I recalled their eerie hooting, those pipes of sound in the silence of the evening farm.

Once out of the avenue, I was immediately under the giant, gnarled Jacaranda trees that imprisoned the house. Here the sun and shade mixed generously together, the white walls of the rondawels dazzling in the sunlight, the faintest blue in shadow.

Thalia immediately came out to greet me. In a few words she would always explain who was there, who was coming, what was happening, what was going to happen. 'Putting one in the picture,' she called it.

'Hail blithest spirit! Hullo, dear.'

Her greetings, her references, were often half-literary, but there was nothing pretentious about Thalia. She had been trained in a good school of journalism and had for years worked on a Fleet Street newspaper. It was when she came to launch a magazine in Johannesburg that I first met her. When the magazine collapsed after a few issues, she decided then to live on her parents' farm. I always thought she was an only child, but it transpired in discussion that she had an obscure brother. It was never made clear by her whether he was still living. In fact, in conversation she would touch on his name very lightly — that is, if she had to

— and then one was aware of the silence that surrounded the reference. She had been on Bloedplaas less than a year when her parents were tragically killed in a car accident. Characteristically enterprising, she tried to farm on her own.

But it didn't work, and large tracts of the farm were sold to meet rising costs, land debts, and income tax until she was left with only a few hundred acres and the idea of her guest house. Still, the whole of the valley and the surrounding mountains remained ours to walk in.

She was now a slender, greying person of some forty-five years, with a great fund of optimism; she was always planning either the running of the guest house, or the extensions of its comforts. For so small and slender a person she produced a surprisingly deep, lovely voice, the South African vocal tones coloured by the precise, though never affected, English accent she had acquired.

'Only one guest at present.' She began 'putting me in the picture.' 'A doctor, she trained at the Johannesburg General, and that's where she is now. A surgeon really.

About thirty-eight. But, in a few days, the place is literally going to overflow. Monica — that's the doctor's name — is having a friend here. And then boys, girls, old and young, stream in. Arts, commerce and science will be represented, so that you'll have a good social field for journalism.'

How good a field, how terrible an assembly, she couldn't of course know. And as well.

She continued putting me in the picture as we walked to the house, I carrying my small bag, Desmond, the house-boy, cook, farm-manager and Jack-of-all-Trades, carrying the larger. In typical South African farm style we would be well tended by servants.

'This is to be your nest.'

She had put me in one of the rondawels on the main square, on its outer edge. I was the first loiterer in the thatch-covered piazza. The two side rondawels were both occupied. Thalia was in one of them permanently. Monica, I understood, was in the other.

'We're having tea now, so don't stay long in your room.'

But it was so delicious being simply there that I felt compelled to pour the jug of soft farm water into the china bowl. (Not hot and cold laid on in the rooms here, Thalia always declaimed.) I wet my face. The room was cool, also twilighty, the floor covered by a thick grass mat bought in Swaziland, the white-washed walls filled with the flower prints Thalia loved so much, and chose and framed so well.

I forgot to tell you that two of the dogs and one of the cats came out with Thalia to welcome me. I should have mentioned them because they are important in the story that follows.

'Tiger' — his tigerishness at the time eluded me, for he appeared gentle and eager — was a massive black and tan Alsatian, with alert, bright eyes, and an enormous, wagging tail. Elsie, incongruously named, was the prima donna of the piece, a red poodle of doubtful temperament, and not at all suited to the rough and tumble of a farm life. The cat that came out was a pearly grey, a prodigy of a fellow, with a mouthful of a name

— 'Liberace' was more often than not abbreviated to an undignified 'Libby'. But he was a boy all right — emasculated by surgery, but masculine assertion otherwise, indifferent to patting, but affectionately responsive in times of silence.

All three were on the stoep to re-welcome me as I opened the bottom half of my door, and stepped out, still lost to the magic of sparkling air. Monica was also there to welcome me, if her cautious, measuring glance could be called that. She was sitting in one of the deep cloth-covered couches that Thalia chose to have on her stoep, reading what seemed a mighty tome of a book. Thalia introduced us. I was surprised at how tall, how strongly slim Monica was, and how reticent. Perhaps she, too, felt that a stranger had come to disturb the silence of paradise. I certainly had felt this about her.

'How do you do?' she said formally, in a rather hard voice. I had the idea that she was nervous and uncomfortable. So was I for that matter, and though, despite my surface easiness, I was always reluctant to meet new people, this particular uneasiness was not quite accountable.

'What's your line?' I asked.

She seemed to resent the question, and replied abruptly, 'Medicine.'

Perhaps she thought I was simply another inquisitive layman. The fact that I was didn't make it any easier.

'I know that. Thalia's told me.' I was equally abrupt. 'You're a general practitioner then?'

She bridled again.

'Oh, dear me no. I do specialise. I'm a thoracic surgeon, with, perhaps necessarily, an interest in pathology on the side. Perhaps you don't know what that is . . . '

She paused uncertainly. In that pause I decided I didn't dislike her completely.

'I had a blood condition once,' I remarked, almost kindly.

'Oh, I see. I really didn't mean to be superior. For some reason women surgeons are still regarded as curious animals.'

Thalia had seen that the conversation had not been of the easy, friendship-making kind she liked at her farm. She hurried on to tell me about the nest a paradise flycatcher had made in one of the surrounding Jacaranda trees. I immediately went out to look at it. When I came back, Desmond had brought tea.

Perhaps I'm given to enthusiasms, but the tea on Thalia's farm tasted as good, as special as everything else she provided. It was served with big, brown-meal scones in which farm butter melted enticingly. We didn't have much to say, all sitting — even Monica had dropped her guard a little — with mouths streaming tea, scone and butter. Easiness restored, Thalia went inside to begin preparations for lunch. Monica returned to her tome. I wandered off in the direction of the dam.

How peaceful it was, half-shadowed by the webbing of Jacaranda, wild fig and Kaffirboom trees. Long yellow reeds threw spear-like shadows over the water which glittered and rippled where it caught the sunlight. The stream from the surrounding hills hissed down to the water, and then made a deeper, melodious sound as it plunged into the depths of the dam. The 'dam', as we called it, was a square pool of rough concrete, about two hundred yards from the house. Looking back you could see the farm-house through the trees, with its six rondawels and the higher thatch of its main rooms. I turned back to the dam, watching some black-faced weavers building their hanging nests and making anxious love to their fussy, hard-to-please hens. In between love and home making they were fighting for territory, ripping up the nest of any neighbour who had come too near for their comfort.

I looked again at the dam, at its deep shadows, and this time a sense touched me, almost like a finger on my back, not of peace, but of apprehension.

★ ★ ★

Lunch was served on the long kiaat table in the main living-room. As usual it was delicious. As usual I ate too much.

The hot, early afternoon was siesta time, and each of us went to our arbours of thatch. I started reading — half-resolving to begin writing in a day or two

— but almost at once I was lulled into a sort of twilight, and drifted into heavy sleep. I had cut the bonds of the city, and here I was gently rocking across the dam. I think I had a boat under me. I tried ineffectively to find out. That was the last thought I had before I became one of the farm's totally inanimate objects.

I woke up some time after four with Desmond bringing tea to my room. I opened the upper half of the door, to look out once more onto paradise. Monica was on the stoep, her head sunk in her tome. Gently I closed the door, and went back to my bed and tea.

My afternoon walk took me up the hills behind the house. Here I renewed my knowledge of the layout of the place. The house couldn't be seen — it was in a cluster of trees, but to the one side of the valley, less than a mile away from Thalia's home I saw the ornate, gabled house belonging to the richest farmer in the district, Mr. Braak. The Braaks scampered after refinement, seldom found it — despite their lavish farm-house that wasn't a farm-house. The gables with the slate roof didn't quite come off. The grapevines refused to grow and the name of the farm, 'The Grapevine', seemed a mockery of its pretensions. The garden was filled with ornaments, concrete dwarfs and toad-stools — a mockery, in turn, of the rugged beauty that surrounded them. 'Wall to wall carpeting inside' I had been told. I preferred the grey cement floors of Thalia's home. Mr. Braak, and his equally pretentious wife, were chagrined about several things that pertained to being Thalia du Mont's neighbours. One was that her cheaply constructed home should call forth the admiration it did, sometimes from distinguished visitors, while theirs, with its gables, elaborate gardens and wall to wall carpeting, should elicit only the admiration of the undistinguished, the unimportant, and — though this did not occur to them — the undiscriminating locals. This ever-present fear of vulgarity is, I suppose, one's own type of snobbery. But I could indulge in a little snobbery while I was on the farm, for Thalia gave herself no airs about the beauty she had created: she loved her home simply and intensely, and enjoyed the love other people felt for it.

The Braaks were always a little piqued, too, about Thalia's name: 'Du Mont' measured up to their sense of refinement, with its suggestion of a French ancestry. 'Braak', by comparison, seemed ugly, and common. Had Thalia been a Braak, the name, I feel, would somehow have acquired splendour.

To the other side of the outcrop of rock on which I stood it was wilder, and here we went for most of our uphill walks. The stream tumbled down a rift in the valley, falling into numerous pools, where we sometimes bathed in the fire-cold water. The threat of bilharzia was not pronounced in this area, and most of the athletic spirits were willing to take the risk. Beyond that was the white sheet of the vlei, which, when the heavy rains came, would turn into a considerable lake, and sometimes made the roads impassable. Behind were the blue mountains of De Kaap — filled with their dreams of lost towns, and deserted diggings. And again in front, on the immediate mountain from which the stream flowed, were the beginnings of the timber world I have mentioned. I hope this picture isn't too confusing, but you have I think the main physical constituents of my story. The Braaks' mansion, grotesquely sedate in its orchards and lawns; Thalia's home in its little wood, with an over-arching avenue of trees; the surrounding mountains and timber; the stream, the vlei, the high splendid sky, the tormenting beauty. It was so desirable it was almost torture to look at it.

I continued my walk, Tiger obediently behind me. He always came with me. We had been joined by one of Thalia's other dogs, a black-haired mongrel stray, 'Waif'. He always saw to it that he looked his part, with his pleading dark eyes, his sad face and hesitantly wagging tail. He looked, particularly when everything was comfortable and happy, as if he expected a disaster at any moment. But at present he was vigorous with life as he ran out in front, tail wagging rapidly, sniffing out koggelmanders and geckoes, sometimes chasing even the birds. The air was alive with silence, and the sounds that came seemed to be played out against this backdrop: the harsh cry of the korhaan, the melancholy throb of the bush-dove — 'my father is dead, my mother is dead, my brothers and sisters are all dead, everyone is dead' is what native legend would have the bush-dove say. Then, disturbing the harsher and sadder cries, the sudden sweet evening song of the African thrush: 'tum, tum, tiddliwinks' repeated again and again, like musical pearls dropped into the bowl of the valley. The shadows had begun to come up across the De Kaap and I knew it was time to go down to the homestead.

My activities for the day were not yet over. Monica was still on the stoep (damn her!), reading her tome. I stripped in my room, and changed into bathing trunks. In a few minutes I was in the dam, its sudden cold, after the hot day, leaving me breathless with pleasure. The coldness seemed to prick deeply into my flesh, and the trees and sky above seemed to grow sharp with the definition of crystal. An extraordinary thing this: the new aspect cold water will give to accustomed objects. When I climbed out my body was highly satisfied. I welcomed the whisky and soda Thalia brought me. We were sitting in the blue shadow of the stoep, the silence seemed even more tangible, and peace had come upon us.

Thalia's low voice broke the silence. 'I must go into town in a moment. My next guest arrives by train.'

'Who is she?' I asked half-resentfully. I could see that Monica also felt something of my resentment. We had both, each a Greta Garbo in our own way, hoped to be alone.

'An old girl called Mrs. Hardwood. Curiously enough, in view of her name, she loves painting trees. None of them much good, I hear. But she likes her hobby, and it fills her life in the absence of Mr. Hardwood, long deceased.'

'Shall I take you to the station?' I offered, half unwillingly, trying to disguise my reluctance. For I hated to go back to a town, having arrived and having begun to absorb the peace of Bloedplaas.

21

'Oh no. I'm geared to this sort of thing.' And, as if sensing my mood, 'You're here for the rest, not to go trundling into sordid urban areas.'

She left soon after that. The hurricane lamps were lit, and threw out squares of orange from the room behind us. We sat in the darkness, not talking, letting the crickets do that for us.

'I love this place.'

Monica interrupted the dark quietness. It was a simple affirmation.

'So do I.'

There seemed no need to say more, but we each had another whisky on it. Contentment, a warmth from my stomach upwards, right up my backbone into my head, was beginning to take over. I wasn't getting drunk, however, except on peace.

Quite soon Thalia's car was swinging back up the avenue — for it was only about an hour to the station and back — the light beaming along the trees, outlining them, creating a huge palisade against the night sky.

We got to our feet to meet Mrs. Hardwood.

She was a heavy-legged, white-haired woman of about sixty-five, spectacled, reserved, awkward. Not fat — but somehow heavy and square on what seemed her tired feet. Those tired feet would, in the week that followed, revive to a terrible energy.

'Glad to meet you.'

She shook hands firmly, yet continued to be awkward and shy. I hoped to myself that we were not going to have a houseful of Monicas and Hardwoods. That would be heavy weather. Yet, and I was to learn my lesson again, for as people relaxed, got to know each other, were tested by the same fires, many good and even splendid things would emerge. Not that all would be splendour at Bloedplaas, by any means.

The conversation was not sparkling, and sometimes we let the heavy night air take over. Mrs. Hardwood described her train journey in uninteresting terms. Monica didn't speak at all. Thalia tried to link up journalism with tree painting and painting with the artistry of surgery. Not with great success, I might say, and yet she attempted it so easily, without affectation or holiday camp-making, because she genuinely was interested in people and their activities, however humble and mundane, however exalted and intricate.

Apart from the heavy night air, and the chirruping of crickets, her mutton and her fine red wine did our talking for us. After coffee we were contented, and happy to go to comfortable chairs under the array of glass-bowled lamps. We read for a while. Monica had under her tome, and was now reading — strange girl! Mrs. Gaskell. Mrs. Hardwood had an Agatha Christie in her hand, but was doing quite a bit of nodding. Thalia and I rustled the newspapers, every now and again making desultory conversation. Tiger, Elsie, Libby, Waif, and the two black cats — Berry and Pitch — were around us.

Suddenly Waif started wailing softly, his voice rapidly becoming louder. Mrs. Hardwood woke with a start. Elsie joined in the wailing, her voice rising to a screeching falsetto . . .

Later that night, in bed, I lay looking up into the thatch. What was it about this visit? What had come to Bloedplaas, or was on its way? What had Waif, with his bitter experience of life, sensed?

The Bushveld night fell over me like a heavy shroud. A sleep of death or not, I was soon asleep.

2

I woke with the sun already in my bedroom. Samantha, the maid, was moving about on the stoep, dusting and tidying. Mrs. Hardwood, who had the rondawel opposite mine, was already up, for looking through the window I saw her moving between the trees, pausing before the waxy white bloom of a magnolia. I wondered when she would begin her painting. Perhaps that would be a signal to me to begin my writing. Monica, no doubt, would go back to her tome on surgery, and think about skilful ways of cutting us up.

I had breakfast in bed, a grand affair, served by Desmond. I didn't think I'd begin my new book that morning.

Indeed, I didn't have much chance because shortly after I got up, two more guests arrived. A married couple; a quiet, colourless accountant, Samuel Smith, and his incessantly talkative wife. If I had regretted Monica and Mrs. Hardwood, how much more I regretted Mrs. Smith. Right from the beginning she spoke about everything and nothing, in a high-pitched, falsetto voice. Thalia was much more adept at making small-talk, but she didn't have a chance against Mrs. Smith's rattle. During tea, she regaled us with the details of her sitting-room furniture. I could see that she thought Thalia's furniture shabby — oh, very quaint and all that, she hastened to qualify — but, now, her ball and claw chairs, these were their features. Mrs. Hardwood was becoming restless — all this talk of furniture; I found her glancing at the trees. So much dead, hard wood this furniture. I smiled at my not very subtle play on her name, saw her glancing up restlessly again, and then, suddenly, liked her and was glad *she* was there.

After that I stopped listening to Charmaine Smith's chatter.

I had left it rather late before I began my morning walk. The sun was hot in the sky. The cicadas were screeching, like the throb of steel. Tiger of course joined me immediately, and I soon saw Waif darting in front. Monica had gone to her bedroom; so, apparently, had Samuel Smith. Mrs. Hardwood was not to be seen. Charmaine, for we had had a bidding to call her this, was telling Thalia about the last church bazaar.

The cicadas were multiplying oppressively, but through the screen of sound, I could hear the usual farm noises, particularly from the valley of the Braaks; the lowing of cattle and the raised voices of the farm workers. A tractor turning. Then I was in the silence of the valley, even the shrilling of the cicadas seeming to have grown faint in the white light that poured over me. I worked my way along the valley, up-stream, pausing every now and again beside a particularly deep pool, watching the white churn of water as it fought its way over the rocks, and hearing its restful chortling as it rolled into the clefts. Sometimes I stopped to examine the patterns on the stone where the water had washed: there were the deep rusts, and also lighter greens and oranges. Surely a potter could here get wonderful ideas for design and colouring?

I looked up quickly, faintly annoyed and puzzled. Waif had begun whimpering again, this time very softly.

A crow, disturbed in the bush, came floating over us, its wings flapping heavily. The cicadas were once again oppressively vocal. The sad sweet voice of the bush-dove spoke up: 'My father is dead . . . Everyone is dead.'

★　★　★

The valley had a haze over it, for I was high above it now. The greens had hardened into greys. The vlei presented a steely blank surface. I should be getting down, if I was to be in time for lunch. I strolled out loose-limbed on the downhill, into the valley, Tiger behind me, Waif darting about in front, his tail wagging vigorously, his nose ecstatically sniffing. Whatever it was that had perturbed him had, apparently, been forgotten.

As I neared the house I saw a figure, heavy-footed, moving in the trees. Mrs. Hardwood. What had made her develop this passion for trees, and what would her paintings be like?

'It's good to be here,' she said, as I came up.

I agreed, and, as with Monica the evening before, it was a real agreement. We were at accord in our love of the farm.

Charmaine was telling a stoically gin-drinking Monica about her family doctor. Samuel Smith was sitting quietly by, sipping a sherry, on the surface listening politely, but not really paying attention.

During lunch Charmaine gave a very vocal recitation of various recipes she knew, but no one was listening, although Mrs. Hardwood was clearly making heavy weather of her indifference. She looked as though she could have clonked Charmaine over the head with a piece of — very hard wood. Really, I chided myself, this tedious play on her name was becoming rather too much. I was here to do some really genuine, if ineffectual, writing.

My self-disgust was arrested for a moment: Thalia was having a quiet, and what appeared an inconsequential discussion with Samuel Smith, and yet she looked puzzled, perhaps even worried. She glanced up from time to time, to look at the madly chattering Charmaine. How those two could have taken to one another was for me a profound mystery. Now Monica was looking at Samuel Smith. Suddenly I felt a curious twinge of resentment. What could they find in that colourless man to interest them, while here was I, the potentially great journalist . . .

My siesta was vaguely troubled on that afternoon. The strong sunlight filtered across my bed and induced a light filled dream. I was under a cap of light, very white light. No, it wasn't even that: I was in the pearly centre of an atom cloud, at the top of the mushroom-like stem. Below me was a long funnel of light, and around me the spreading canopy of pearly cloud. Then darkly a figure hovered on the edge of the dome, throwing a minute but unmistakable shadow. The shadow was looking at me. I woke up with the oppressed feeling of having been watched.

I was greeted by the sunlight streaming through the windows and the open top half of the door. Everything was in order. The big chest of drawers was squarely facing me, with all its various contents stowed neatly away. I was reminded of a sketch I had written on my last visit, in which I tried to express the sort of delicious story each drawer had to tell about its contents. But now my translation was wider: Thalia had brought together into her house a variety of human suit-cases, each one neat on the surface, but with its own story, and its own secret compartments. Still more suit-cases would be arriving. Was it this that filled me with apprehension, with a foretaste of excitement and adventure?

I still had the feeling of oppression when I got up. I didn't go for my walk today, decided instead to swim off the feeling of heaviness. Monica had gone to fetch a friend from the station, a young school-teacher who would be sharing her rondawel. Samuel Smith and Mrs. Hardwood were still apparently sleeping, but I heard Charmaine's high voice from the kitchen giving tips on savoury-making. The deeper, truer melody of Thalia's voice was washed towards me now and again.

I walked slowly down to the dam, stripping to my bathing shorts. Sitting half in sharp sunlight, half in dappled shadow, I dangled my feet in the water, listening to the gush of the feed pipe. For a quick second, silence struck out at me.

I wasn't alone. Mrs. Hardwood wasn't in her bedroom. She was in the shadowy trees below the dam, watching me. But she was also working, for I saw the easel beside her. I should have put some clothes on, or perhaps I should not have forced myself on her. But I sauntered across in my half-dressed condition, highly curious. I must see what her drawings were like.

As I came up she said, very simply:

'Would you like to see my work?' and then added with a genuine diffidence: 'Such as it is.'

Yet the sketch on her easel was surprisingly good. Three or four trees were in it, imparting their native strength:

on the edge were the shadowy forms of Jacarandas and London planes; at the centre the stark, knotty form of an almost leafless Kaffirboom. This tree was filled out in strong spare lines. But what intrigued me was the suggestion of water below the trees, and on the edge, the shadowy form, only a few quick strokes, of a human figure. The figure seemed to 'place' the trees, the scene. It wasn't the stock use of the human form as a focusing device, for whoever it was, seemed a ghost, the spirit of the place, filled with the spirit of water and the trees.

She saw me looking at the figure.

'That's you,' she said. 'I knew something was missing in my picture, and I only had time to get a few lines as you sat there.'

I was a naked ghost, the shadowy embodiment of the place. Perhaps as I looked at other people, so they looked at me.

'It's excellent,' I said referring to the picture.

'It has poor lines,' she admitted without

trying to be demure. 'But then I'm not a professional. I believe a professional painter is coming tomorrow, so Miss du Mont tells me. But you thought, didn't you, I'd draw awful, stilted rubbish.'

'No — not at all,' I murmured untruthfully.

But I wasn't convincing, and Mrs. Hardwood smiled her slow smile, as though she were in pain.

'Well, I'll get back to the water,' I tapered off, annoyed at my awkwardness.

I dived in immediately, and the cold breaking liquid was relief, as though an abnormal pressure had been released. It was wonderfully exhilarating as the white fire of the water tore along my flanks. I didn't want to be old, or middle-aged — but young. Looking over the edge of the pool I saw Mrs. Hardwood at her drawing once again, and I realised that she wasn't really old. Her eagerness made her young; she was younger than Charmaine, who had no sense of wonder, whose life seemed a steady parade of known, easily-mastered things, recipes and curtains, snacks and ball-and-claw furniture. Perhaps after all, there wasn't much in *her* suit-case.

But the snacks she had made for us to have with our evening drinks were very good: the hollowed eggs piled with caviare, the little biscuits tipped with anchovy. I was at peace, and purred over my whisky and soda. I didn't even mind Charmaine, in fact quite liked her and her quiet husband. He was giving Thalia advice about her account-keeping.

It was then that Moncia arrived with her companion, Judith. She was an incredibly lovely girl, of about thirty-one or thirty-two. She had that rare blue-black sort of hair and a fair skin, and moved with a confident grace, a sway of the hips that was altogether enchanting. Thalia told me a little about her: she was a divorcee of some two years' standing, a teacher, possessed, I have no doubt, of considerable grace and wit. She was totally unlike the angular Monica, who was her elder by several years. How their friendship came into being was one of those secrets of life's chest of drawers. And yet there was a likeness, not in any action or physical line or colouring; it was a delicate, teasing sense of affinity.

Judith dropped gracefully into a chair, accepted the whisky and soda that was brought to her by Monica, and fitted easily into the pattern of conversation. For a moment Charmaine's babbling was stilled by the elegant music of the girl. I could see she fascinated Monica; even Thalia, that impresario of interesting visitors, even Samuel Smith, who seemed to show interest in so very little, were looking at her observantly.

'What a hot, tiring train journey, but what remarkable scenery!'

I could see Mrs. Hardwood hovering on the outer circle of these much younger visitors. Then Thalia with her relaxed courtesy included her in the conversation, in the circle sitting in the darkening twilight. She gave her a sherry to sip.

'We came through Waterval Boven and Onder — an enchanting valley,' Judith was saying. 'We must travel around a bit, Monica, while we are here. The old mining towns, for example. I hear the scenery in the forest world, and that at

Graskop and the Blyde River Canyon, are simply marvellous.'

'Simon knows that part of the world well,' said Thalia, referring the conversation to me.

'Oh,' said Judith, perhaps really looking at me for the first time. 'Do you come from this part of South Africa.'

I felt annoyingly diffident as I replied:

'No, I'm a journalist, and I write about the Eastern Transvaal. A long story of fascination.'

'Oh, but I know you!' She looked at me eagerly now. 'At least your books. You're Simon Digby, the well-known author.'

'I'm flattered that you put it that way,' I said lamely, again annoyed at my awkwardness.

'Do you think you could bear to go again, and introduce us to this part of the world?'

'I'd like to,' I said, and then had the oddest sensation, amounting to resentment, that, apart from Thalia and myself, someone present knew this world well, and wasn't saying so. The knowledge sat silently with me, another of those interesting but irritating signals I had received on this holiday.

Or perhaps it was knowledge that was coming, that was stalking up to us in the form of the last two visitors . . . I thought then of the two guests who would complete the party. Two young men, I had been told by Thalia. The one an artist and art-teacher. The younger, an embryo scientist.

'Perhaps we should wait until the party's complete,' I said. My words fell into the dusk.

'Yes,' said Thalia. 'The two young men come tomorrow, and I think Eric Shackleton — he's the artist — knows part of this world. I've certainly seen a drawing of his of God's Window.'

'That's near Graskop, isn't it?' said Mrs. Hardwood. Was she stating a fact or asking a question? I couldn't be sure.

But what the hell did it matter if anyone *did* know this part of the world well? I couldn't reserve the priorities for myself. My books were intended to introduce people to the splendours and mysteries of the Eastern Transvaal. I had to try not to be one of those literary frauds who want their books to be a substitute for the actual thing.

'The Kruger Game Reserve is also nearby,' said Mrs. Hardwood, this time stating a fact.

She wanted, it seemed, to see these places, but didn't have a car.

We had another drink. The stars were beginning to come out. The Laughing Doves were having their last rustle and murmur before settling in the trees above us. The crickets had begun, and also a thousand other minute farm noises, like pricks of sound in the night. Despite the presence of several other people it was deeply satisfying.

The storm and gas lanterns were being lit, and shadows and lights formed in the little group. Thalia's dark eyes looked deeper for the light showing the blank whiteness of her face. The planes of Judith's remarkable features were caught. Mrs. Hardwood sat in shadow. Samuel Smith blinked uncomfortably in the full light that caught him. Charmaine looked bewildered at her inability to get into the conversation.

Then the cowbell rang, and that was Desmond's signal for dinner.

Afterwards we sat reading, except Charmaine, who was playing a grotesque game of Honeymoon Bridge with her husband. Thalia was restless and would walk out into the night every now and again, looking up at the stars as if for guidance.

I caught her on one of these occasions, and tried to be jocularly abrupt.

'What's up?'

'I don't know,' she hesitated. 'I'm usually quite confident about these gatherings, but this time . . . Call it premonition, foreboding. Oh dear, here I am trying to spoil my own magic world and, into the bargain, my own custom. Don't worry about the musings of old Auntie Thalia.'

We went inside. Judith had gone to bed. Monica was closing her medical dictionaries. Mrs. Hardwood was knitting suddenly like a crab possessed. Mrs. Smith was chattering at her quietly assenting husband.

I said goodnight, taking my lantern with me. I turned it off very soon after getting into bed, and slept a dreamless sleep.

*   *   *

Our last two house guests arrived from Johannesburg early that morning. I was still in bed, but I glimpsed one of them as he came from the car-port, suit-case in hand: scimitar thin, a blade of a man, with blond, wavy hair, and rather a flat, high-pitched voice. I didn't see the other member of the party, but I heard his voice, which was youthful, sharply keen. He was quite a few years younger than his companion, I calculated.

I had breakfast again in bed that morning and lingered over my steaming black coffee, and the opening chapter I was trying to compose.

Finally I decided I wasn't satisfied with it, for I jumped up impatiently and dressed quickly. The two new arrivals were having breakfast on the stoep when I came out of my rondawel. They were eating their paw-paw with gusto when I appeared on the scene, but jumped up diligently as Thalia began her ceremony of introduction. The scimitar like man was rather younger than I, about thirty-three, thirty-four I guessed. Seeing him stirred my memory, and I remembered that Eric Shackleton was, in fact, a well-known Johannesburg artist. His companion was, as I had guessed, considerably younger, not much more than twenty-two. He was shorter than the six foot plus Eric, more compact. Indeed, although sensitive in appearance, was sturdily put together. His face was that extraordinarily touching mixture of youthful ruggedness and delicate good looks. Eric Shackleton's hair was of the stiff wavy kind that off-set his sharp features: Anthony Reade's soft hair seemed to be a shadow to the beauty of his face.

Quite a few things struck me. One was that he was in fact much younger than everyone else, and I wondered whether he would like it. The other thought struck me almost simultaneously: he would find a match in looks in Judith, and they would be either rival darlings or get on well together. There was also a weird sort of similarity in the set-up, a male couple, a female couple. The younger male under the protection of an older male, and move the age register up a bit: a young female under the protection of an older female.

Then I found myself pleased to have not only these young, handsome people about, but someone of the calibre of Eric Shackleton. I remembered more and more of his pictures, and knew that I liked them. Under the sharpness of his manner there was an insight, a compassion, that would make him, I thought, a great artist.

Judith then came out, looking self-possessed and elegant in slacks. She was introduced and, with relief and well-being, I saw that neither she nor Eric nor Anthony were going to be rivals. Almost instantly the company had become exhilarating. I might really be able to write something worthwhile that holiday.

The high, fluting tones of Charmaine disturbed the morning air.

3

Something rather amusing — almost beautiful — happened later that morning. Mrs. Hardwood had been introduced to Eric as a fellow artist, and over morning tea, in a somewhat forbidding manner, he was questioning her about her work. She, nervous with diffidence, had assumed a defensive truculence. The discussion between the artists wasn't going well.

'Oh come, Mrs. H,' said Thalia, with her usual ease. 'Let Eric see some of your drawings.'

'Not for the world.'

'He'll tell you what they're worth.'

'That's what I'm afraid of. I know he'll be perfectly honest. Illusions are good sometimes.'

'But your drawings are good,' I said.

Eric looked at me with interest. I could see that he had heard of me, perhaps read some of my books, and that he set some store by my opinion.

His manner towards Mrs. Hardwood softened a little.

'Come on, let's see your drawings. Don't be so coy. In return I'll let you see some that I'm working on.'

Without protesting again she went to collect her work, and he turned to the sketching block that lay beside him.

Charmaine was looking bored. Samuel was reading an out-of-date newspaper. Monica, inevitably, was lost in the by-ways of surgery. Judith and Anthony (or 'Tony', as most of them called him) were looking at a bird manual, trying to identify the birds that fluttered out of the surrounding trees. The animals lolling beside us, Tiger and Waif, waited for their walk.

Mrs. Hardwood returned with her sketch-book, her face slightly red. She was flustered by her sudden emergence into the art world.

She sat next to Eric, and abruptly opened her book. I looked on from the other side. She started off with plantations of pine trees and blue-gums, some of them filled in in great detail, but their colour often suggested only by the faintest, the most subtle of green washes. Then there were individual trees: one not very successful magnolia, with a cream wash to suggest its flower; the wild fig, drawn with greater care, but rather more stilted. The Jacarandas and London planes were better again, and at the end, she showed him her sketch of the Kaffirboom, where I was the ghost.

'What sort of pictures do you make?' she asked anxiously, for he had said little about her drawings, only grunting faintly every now and again.

'I like these,' he said curtly. 'Some of them are good, really good.'

Mrs. Hardwood coloured even more deeply. She was suffused with the pleasure his unexpected praise had given.

'Do you mean that?'

'I wouldn't say it otherwise.'

'And your pictures?' she reminded him.

'I'm off scenery at present,' he said. 'I'm doing the human figure mainly.'

'You said you'd let me look at them, in return . . . '

'Here some of them are,' he responded

carelessly, flicking open his sketching block. 'These are pictures of Tony.'

I saw Mrs. Hardwood turn pale and then colour even more vividly, deeper than any hue she had yet assumed. I glanced down at the sketching block. This drawing was one of Tony done from the front, the eyes of the boy on those of the artist. The figure was stark naked. There was no attempt at concealment.

'This is another of Tony.'

He flicked over the page, and here Tony was, again naked, drawn from the side, his buttocks looping gracefully out, his eyes fixed on the invisible horizon.

And yet another of the naked young visitor, this one of him sitting down, smiling, again no attempt at disguise, his figure seeming to assume a graceful innocence.

If Eric had noticed Mrs. Hardwood's embarrassment, he didn't show it. In fact I don't think he did notice it. He was treating her simply as a fellow artist, and this was really the greatest compliment he could have paid her.

But at present Mrs. Hardwood was

rather too confused to notice subtle compliments.

I glanced across at the subject of her embarrassment, but Tony and Judith were still paging through the bird-book, their heads bent over it.

Eric had none of Mrs. Hardwood's reticence about asking for an opinion of his work.

'How do you like them?'

'Well . . . ' Mrs. Hardwood was dreadfully self-conscious, and then, perceptibly gathering her strength, she made a decision. 'I think they're very fine. I'm old-fashioned, but I do like them.'

'I'm glad,' said Eric, and he seemed to mean this. I was taking to him more and more.

Thalia had picked up the sketching block.

'But these are of you, Tony, and you're naked!'

Judith had now come across, and the inspection of Tony's nudity had become quite a general thing. Except for charmaine. She had got up and gone to her bedroom, visibly annoyed at this vulgar intrusion on tea and cakes, curtaining and carpets. But Samuel had also looked at the drawings, and seemed vaguely to approve.

Mrs. Hardwood sat on stoically. It required all the courage of her sixty-five years to do so, but I could see that somewhere she had been touched. She had become a fellow artist.

Thalia was now inspecting her drawings.

'But these are incredibly good, Mrs. H.'

Judith and Tony liked them too, and with their approval I felt that the warmth and genuineness of the party had been established. This would be no mere brandy-drinking gathering.

We then began to talk of the trip we were to embark on the next morning. This would take us through the timber world of Sabie, through to the next valley of the ghost hamlet, Pilgrim's Rest.

Tony and Eric, Judith and I then went for a quick bathe in the dam, and when we came out of our white fire or champagne (whichever way you choose to look at it) it was lunch-time.

And I'm going to try not to tell you about any of Thalia's memorable meals.

★　★　★

In the late afternoon I looked for my walking companions, Tiger and Waif, but they had gone off — so a subdued Charmaine told me — with Tony and Judith, who had arranged to walk up-stream, towards the source. Eric was away drawing and I could see Mrs. Hardwood, sitting below the dam, her sketching block on her knees.

I felt curiously deserted, particularly by Tiger and Waif. Elsie could not be induced to move a single paw.

I decided not to climb, or to go up-stream, but to go down to the vlei that had glittered like sheet-metal when I had seen it on my day of arrival.

The track twisted down, past some of the Braak's sheds, and soon became boggy. If the rains came with any abruptness and force there was often an unexpected piling up of water here. The cattle egrets were winging overhead, coming in to roost among the reeds and on the old twisted branches of trees that stuck out above the water. The black-faced weavers were creating their usual clatter as they worked at their dark-entranced nests hanging over the water. Their quarrelling and sense of competition were prodigious. Some of the more brazen birds would rip open a rival's nest when he was off gathering grass. Some of them perched on the top of the long bamboo leaves, deftly tore them right down for two feet or so, and then came sailing over, streaming the long shreds like gay banners. It was a stirring sight. But I warned you, didn't I, that there would be much that was stirring on Thalia's farm?

Only the sluggish water between the reeds seemed to suggest something more sinister. Was it danger? Again, ridiculously, the back of my neck began to crawl, and I realised that evening — a grey, thin evening — was drawing in. The reeds were throwing shadowy reflections across the vlei.

The world seemed to sigh, to draw an

enormous, apprehensive breath. In the grass and mud beneath I saw the curving body of a snake, weaving its brilliant way towards the water, its back a dangerous green. I didn't feel fear. Such an unelaborately beautiful thing — no excrescences of legs and arms, just sheer body moving behind a prodding head.

The sunlight was rippling across in little bobs and glints of light, and fear drew even further off. I was once again flooded with a sense of well-being. Thalia, Mrs. Hardwood, Eric, Tony, Judith — how substantial they seemed as people. Then, with a slight shock, I realised that there had been exclusions. I consoled myself as I trudged homeward. One couldn't like everybody, and I didn't actually *mind* the others.

It seemed as though I had been at Bloedplaas a long time — not simply three days — and had known them all a long time. How little I knew of them I was to find out.

I had not seen the farm at its angriest.

★　★　★

Monica had unbent a little and I saw, with something approaching relief, that after supper she cast her medical tome to one side and began to read the Agatha Christie Mrs. Hardwood had abandoned. That was more like it, I thought to myself. She's beginning to thaw. It was clear that there was a very affectionate bond between herself and Judith, for they made some remarks about their city lives that showed compassionate understanding by each of the other's purposes.

Charmaine had begun to question Judith about her life. Didn't she find it lonely? Could she really take to teaching, having once been married?

I could see the question hovering on Charmaine's lips.

What had he been like?

Everyone was waiting for the question. But it wasn't asked.

Eric was drawing under one of the lamps, and I saw the sketches of the group of people around him. Mrs. Hardwood abstractedly gazing out of the window, her spectacles lit with the flame of one of the lamps. It was evident that

Eric, too, saw something, a concealed strength, in the old woman. There was a quick drawing of Monica and Judith, with their heads turned to one another. Yet another of Judith and Tony, their heads bowed over a book. I saw that Eric had not missed the morning's tableau.

What also enchanted me was that Tony, so much younger than anyone else, wasn't bored, and that Mrs. Hardwood, so much older, wasn't either, and, even more intriguing, that she had taken a vivid liking to the boy. This young sapling had, for her, the making of a good tree.

She decided to treat herself to a round of patience, and Thalia spread a table for her. Charmaine was all for playing rummy, having recovered her brightness. It was her unassuming husband who turned away from the prospect, I think because he saw just how aghast we were.

'But I like rummy!' she protested.

'I'll play a round of Honeymoon Bridge with you tonight in the rondawel,' he suggested patiently.

'Oh, all right! But what are we to do now?'

'Talk,' said Monica, looking up from her book, and having set so poor an example.

Charmaine was not so obtuse not to have seen this.

'Well, you're a fine one, I must say! With your nose glued to a book, usually a medical rigmarole with hideous pictures. I've looked at them. How a woman can bring herself to do that kind of job is beyond me.'

Monica got up, cool rather than calm, and walked out under the stars. Judith immediately followed her.

'Well, I hope I haven't done anything now!' said Charmaine crossly. 'I only said . . . '

'Say no more, dear,' said Samuel, and put his hand gently on hers.

She accepted his consolation.

I looked at Eric's sketch block.

There were a few quick lines of a grimacing Charmaine, and then from a quiet body, came the strong head of her husband. This sketch seemed more sociological than compositional. My admiration for Eric, as an artist, and as a person of insight, increased once again.

That night the pearly cloud of my dream had become dark shadows, and I saw two women wandering together under the stars. They were joined by a third person, and someone else was looking at them. Then the three were two again, and I couldn't tell whether they were men or women. This distressed me, and I woke myself with a whimper that resembled Waif's.

★ ★ ★

This was not a hot day, but a day wreathed in fog, as if someone had silently let a shroud drop over us. Sounds clinked and tinkled and had altogether a special resonance. A good day for travelling, I told myself, as long as we'd be able to see something at the end of it all.

The timber world, which lay on the edge of Thalia's valley, was covered by mist, each tree drawing its chiffon veil about it. We were travelling in two cars, mine and Eric's. Thalia had elected to go with Mrs. Hardwood in Eric's car. The Smiths had joined them.

Monica and I sat in front, Judith and Tony behind. The car nosed up the splendid tarred roads, in and out of pine forests. Sometimes, as low cloud came swirling across, we could see little more than two yards in front of us. My headlights picked oddly at the wraith-like vapours that gathered.

It was, of course, very atmospheric and we all felt it.

'I wonder whether Eric will be able to draw this,' said Tony, almost musing to himself.

'This!' said Monica archly, amused at the absurdity of the proposition. 'It's only grey mist . . . Nothing else.'

'Yes, but he can do just about anything with pencil and paint.'

I realised the extent to which Tony believed in a great artist, and felt a stab of jealousy for the esteem Eric commanded.

The fog cleared slightly as we drove into Sabie, a little town clustered in a dense timber world. For a moment we saw Eric's car ahead with its five occupants, Thalia in front talking to Eric, Charmaine, it seemed, talking to everyone. Her husband and Mrs. Hardwood were silent listeners.

'I have the funniest sensation,' said Judith suddenly, 'that all is not what it seems.'

Monica turned on her sharply. She spoke with an edge to her voice.

'What do you mean by that, Judith?'

The girl giggled self-consciously.

'For the moment I'm not saying.'

'I hate mysteries!' her companion responded crossly. I felt that more than this she resented Judith's sudden friendship with Tony.

But we were now out of Sabie, and picking our way through timber forests towards Pilgrim's Rest. Looking through my notes I see I've mentioned Pilgrim's Rest before, that strange ghost town of about a hundred residents, perhaps the most important of all the early gold settlements of South Africa. As we neared the town the hill-sides became mysteriously groined with the primitive diggings of the early pioneers. Timber would give way to the rivulets and potholes of panners; small corrugated iron dwellings would speak of less polished eras.

I love Pilgrim's Rest, and have always said that if I had to leave the ambitious pother of Johannesburg, this is where I'd come. One reason was to be near Bloedplaas, another to be in a quiet, backwater place of few people but a thousand memories, and twice as many ghosts. The modern road to Pilgrim's Rest was a well-made one where we turned sharply up from the highway.

But we had now crossed to the other side of the hill, and were descending into a closed-in valley. The conversation, inevitably, turned to gold.

'What were those descriptions of gold diggings in our room?' Monica asked Judith.

'Thalia lent them to me to look at. I'm trying to compile some sort of record, and pursue a particular whimsy I have.'

'Anything serious wouldn't interest you, of course.'

Monica's words were characteristically abrupt. As so often before, they verged on rudeness.

'The only things that interest you are medical works. About anything else you know very little.'

The retort was equally sharp, and it was deserved. The pause was uncomfortable. Then Judith turned to me.

'As a writer I think you'd be interested in my little line,' she said. 'Part of it may in fact turn out to be a personal interest.'

'I'd like to see what you have found,' I answered. 'Thalia has always kept her archives hidden from me. I think she still supects me, perhaps rightly, of being a nosy journalist. I'd like to discuss your findings with you.'

How near I was running to danger I was not to know. Only tragedy would prevent a discovery that might have put us all on our guard.

Pilgrim's Rest was virtually a one street village, most of the buildings consisting of peeling corrugated iron structures. The hotel was also made of corrugated iron, its bar, dating from mining days, was an iron chapel towed up from Moçambique, here to satisfy something other than the religious needs of the miners. I looked to right and left, bemusedly trying to choose a shack for my retirement; all the houses were dismally, quaintly similar, with a sad, scratched air about them, fit only for the habitation of mining ghosts.

'The past is here,' said Judith with a pleasant solemnity.

The car in front had stopped, and we saw Eric doing a few lightning sketches. Mrs. Hardwood watched him intensely, admiringly.

'He'll get something good here,' said Tony, with an admiration equal to Mrs. Hardwood's. Again that pang of jealousy for the artist who was recognised. Yet, I mused, looking for a self-satisfaction I was far from feeling, in my own field some people would remember me.

We passed Eric's car and left the tarred road. The valleys became empty of trees, but they were quite as beautiful. A tranquil sense of desolation descended on us, and the throbbing, harsh cry of the turtle dove became the pulse of our mood. In a way it was delicious.

The dirt road continued for about twenty miles, and at some stages was difficult to negotiate. It was no surprise that so few tourists had attempted this particular route. We were now in a native reserve area, the hillsides dotted with groups of huts and small mud houses; there was a signal scarcity of signposts. It was as well that I knew what we were looking for. I stopped at the beginning of the tarred road, parked under the blue-gum trees and waited for the other car to arrive. We were going to see Bourke's Potholes, a series of vast pools eroded in the rocks.

We were joined by the second car, and the nine of us walked down towards the river. There had been some division of ranks, for Mrs. Hardwood was very much on her own, and showed no inclination to join Samuel, whose wife was firmly leached onto Thalia. Eric joined Monica and Tony, and Judith, for some reason, chose to walk ahead with me.

'You know, it wasn't simply curiosity,' she announced.

I thought she was referring to her curiosity about Bourke's Potholes.

'No, I don't mean this.' She brushed

the spectacle aside. 'I mean my interest in the area and the people who lived here. Their ghosts fascinate me. I divorced my husband, I think you know that.'

The change of direction was once again unexpected.

'He came from these parts. When Monica spoke of a holiday it was my idea that we should come here.'

We were interrupted, dramatically and inarguably, by the Potholes below us, like so many round, ill-fitting pieces in a puzzle. Judith had presented me with a number of jagged bits that wouldn't fit, no matter how much you pushed them together. What could all these odd references mean — prospectors, husbands, ghosts?

The Potholes had to be crossed and re-crossed by several, apparently fragile, aluminium bridges. As I stood on one watching the water, a skeletal finger ran itself down my backbone. Again I was possessed with foreboding and misgiving. Were these people what they seemed? Mrs. Hardwood, now standing on her own, a solitary figure on one of the bridges? I even felt uncertain about Thalia, about the unknown areas of her life. Charmaine, it seemed, had managed to say something that made her restive. Were these undercurrents actual, or only the product of an over-busy imagination?

Eric was behind me with his sketch block, and I caught a glimpse of his drawings, the smooth-walled holes dropping down, like glass, into the turbulent waters — but a figure took up the foreground, an anonyomus, sexless, faceless figure, its back to us, looking at the turmoil and, somehow apart from it, part of it. Eric had stood behind me. Was this again myself? Was I doomed to play the role of a spectator at life's feast? I didn't much fancy the idea.

Lunch was taken at the corrugated iron hotel of Pilgrim's Rest. It was a happy enough party that sat down to it. Eric was being very nice to Mrs. Hardwood. Thalia at last was with someone other than Charmaine, though, alas, I was now engaged with the latter. Monica and Samuel Smith seemed to have got into conversation. As we had our drinks in the lounge, some of the young men who still helped to mine the depleted diggings came into the chapel bar and their lively, raucous voices cut across the ghosts of the morning, and dismissed them.

I, too, was happy. The dining-room was a medium-sized hall with long tables covered by fresh white cloths and an abundance of flowers. The wine was good, the meal well cooked, and conversation began to flow.

4

Bed came early that night. The next morning dawned golden. Surely there could be nothing wrong with this world? Thalia herself brought in my breakfast.

'It was a good day, wasn't it?' I knew that this wasn't simply assertion. It was Thalia's need for confirmation. She herself seemed to be glowing, as though good things were about to happen to the world.

'Yes.' It seemed to require only that.

'You know, at one time I was worried,' she went on. 'This seemed such an odd pottage of people. Yet they are fitting in, even Chatterbox and silent Scrooge.'

'Why Scrooge?'

'Well, he's an accountant and they are reputedly mean. I think Mrs. Hardwood adores Eric.'

'Yes.' Again the pang of jealousy.

'But I think, my sweet, she likes you even better.'

'Nonsense!' My jealousy was replaced by the annoyingly boyish embarrassment that plagued me. And pleasure. I wanted to count with Mrs. Hardwood.

'She's got one of your books in her room. I saw it when I went in to say goodnight, yesterday evening. I think she got it when we stopped at Sabie. She went into the booksellers then.'

'Which book is it?'

'That one about the mystery of the diggings and Blyde.'

I was putting egg into my mouth as we spoke. She was sitting on the edge of my bed, and the feeling of comfortableness returned.

Nothing, nothing could affect this brilliant sense of peace. Even the sapphire winged kingfisher that came to sit on the wooden frame of my open window seemed to confirm the shimmering sparkle of my joy, and of the world outside. The lawn glittering with dew, and the trees lacing the landscape were signals of peace.

'And Monica?' I asked.

'She's good,' Thalia said.

Even this seemed acceptable today.

The peace of the morning was not to stay intact. The Braaks chose this as the day for their State Visit. They came down out of their stylish, Dutch-gabled house and imposed themselves on Thalia and her company. Everyone seemed to be around to be introduced to ruddy-complexioned, pot-bellied Mr. Braak and his stiff-backed, hard faced wife. Tiger whined softly, cheated of his walk. Elsie had hysterics. The Braaks thought Thalia made far too much of her animals, and they were openly contemptuous of the morning's performances.

'Ach,' said Mrs. Braak, 'you must smarten up your house, Talie, if you're going to have so many people to stay.'

Despite her apparent pompousness, there was a direct earthiness about her speech that was not unattractive.

'Yes, man,' confirmed her husband with quite as much decision, 'you should go to see old Smit, the contractor in town. He'll be able to give you tips about lighting and breaking down walls.'

'I don't want to break down walls, or to

have too much light,' Thalia reminded him.

The Braaks looked disgusted. They never could understand mysteries, had no time for them. If people wanted to live like pigs . . . They didn't care — and yet they cared terribly, for here was a world which had, they felt instinctively, some superiority to their own, but which they just couldn't understand.

'I believe you draw pictures?' said Mrs. Braak, turning to Eric.

'Yes, but nudes, mainly.'

'Ach, man!' said Mr. Braak, faintly embarrassed by dirty talk in mixed company.

'Oh, Talie, I heard something funny from one of the farm natives,' said Mrs. Braak, turning away from the blind alley of nudes to local gossip that would interest Thalia. 'He said the ghost was back in the valley. He saw it from a hill, and knew it was a spirit.'

'Who?' Thalia's voice was sharp. I was suddenly reminded of the obscure brother. Was he alive or dead, and, to be fanciful, was his ghost in the valley, flitting from shade to shade! Yet he had, I believe, been an amiable, object-free person. I was aware that everyone was listening. They had sensed it, then? Judith's eyes seemed to me particularly bright, but then, perhaps, I'm still in retrospect, trying to fit my jigsaw together.

Mrs. Braak took her time in answering Thalia's question, savouring her news.

'I don't know. But it's funny isn't it? You know, Talie, I think he was on his way back from a beer drink. He reeked, honestly.'

Mr. Braak was telling Tony, the scientist, about his technically superb approach to farming, in contrast to people who didn't know anything about it . . . The implied reference was not at all discreet, for even Thalia's parents had been foolish people, who saw their farm as a joy. It was a badly paying one, true; but to them it was not a conveyer belt proposition. Mr. Braak couldn't, it seemed to my amused mind, bring himself to talk to Eric again after his reference to naked dames. Drawing was scenery, man, and perhaps a picturesque kaffir or two — but that was all.

Tony's responses were sufficiently practical.

'Have you tried N.K. fertiliser?'

'Man, but it's strong. We don't want to kill that ghost in the valley, you know!'

The joke wasn't feeble. Yet it fell on a curious silence. Even Mr. Braak realised it, and he looked at the company with something approaching dismay.

Everyone was now in the cocoon of his own thought. Every one a drawer with his own paraphernalia piled into it. Mrs. Hardwood and her trees. Judith and her absent husband. The incongruous Smiths. But I mustn't go on spotlighting people in this manner, for they all seemed, in some way or other, to repulse the bright beams placed on them. The Braaks were a signal of brash daylight, and even brash daylight was something to be feared by those who lived in the shadows.

★   ★   ★

Luckily the Braaks didn't stay too long once they had gulped their tea. Although the morning was hot, we soon busily dispersed to our various activities. Judith and Tony had already disappeared. Mrs. Hardwood carried her folding canvas stool into the trees. Tiger and Waif were whimpering for a walk. I soon set off.

The cicadas were at their shrill labour. The veld seemed alive with underground activity. I crossed the main vegetable field of the Braaks, where the black women could be seen with their hoes cleaning and irrigating. The day had become intensely hot. The clouds forming in the sky were like magnificent cabbages or balloons.

I was bound for one of the more immediate hills, which would permit a view across the valleys of De Kaap as far as the timber world. It was heavy going, first through the long, khaki grass now greening into the sweetness of summer, and then across the rocks, and then, finally, with a burst of triumph, onto the crest of the hill where the world — the secret world of bushes and dwellings — lay exposed below. The dogs came padding behind, their lolling tongues bobbing with their panting. Once at the top, I lay back contentedly. Tiger sat surveying the world beyond.

Apparently without reason he began whimpering. That odd sixth sense stirred the skin across my scalp. I sat up, my straining eyes searching the veld. I could see nothing unusual in a countryside where there was so much to see, so many hazy activities, the black women — minute figures now — in the brown-ridged fields, the thin threads of spiralling smoke, the dense bushes.

Then I saw why Tiger had been disturbed. Little more than a dot of a figure was in the fields far below. For no ostensible reason, there was something sinister about its movements. I couldn't even tell whether it was male or female, but somehow the posture, the creeping through the grass, was that of a vicious animal. I wished I had brought my field glasses with me. If only I had, the mystery of the Braak valley would perhaps have been solved and tragedy averted. But this is conjecture.

For a moment I was frightened to

move, and then, danger acting like a magnet, I knew that truth, honour, curiosity, or simply the mesmerism of my fear, must make me follow. I got up, Tiger still whimpering, descended as quickly as I could. My nervousness made me clumsy. I stumbled once or twice, and on one occasion slipped badly, rocking down the face of a fortunately now gentle hill. When I recovered myself, nothing was to be seen and I had lost all sense of direction. Precisely where the creature had been moving I simply did not know.

I moved across the valley towards the stream. I had hurt myself rather badly and wanted to clean away the blood on my hands. I came on the water at a narrow point and, among the ferns and bracken, knelt down and let the crystal gurgle wash off the red clutter. The water was cool and soft, whispering through my fingers, telling me of peace in the soft tremble of its music, the deep fluting of its waterbirds. Then slowly I moved up-stream, for the moment having forgotten my ghost and my fear, feeling little else but the soft joy of the water. The dogs were padding silently beside me.

As we neared the bigger pools I realised that we were not alone, for I heard the soft, confidential stirring of voices. The presence of my ghost re-asserted itself, and so I moved quietly to the bushes overhanging the pool from where I had heard murmuring. Perhaps the answer to my mystery was here. I quietly pushed aside the shrubs and looked down at the pool.

The ghost wasn't there, but I was hardly less surprised by what I did see. Judith and Tony were standing beside the pool, both of them naked.

They were knee-deep in water, the sunlight smoothing down their skins. It seemed so overpoweringly innocent, so beautiful, their delicate nymph-like bodies beginning to probe the delicious coldness of the pool. They were both splendidly lithe, well-formed creatures. Judith, her dark hair off-set by the ivory of her body, the fair mounds of her breasts, and below the curve of her stomach, the dark triangle. Tony seemed to be very much like the sketches Eric had made of him, but within the form of his youthful slenderness he had become a young god alive, his golden brown hair glittering in the sun, nesting over the shadow of a face intent on the pool beneath him. His chest curved down gracefully into the hard mushroom of his stomach, and then, around his loins, into the firm gentle strength of his thighs.

They seemed like two sun-creatures searching the water.

Then they held hands, laughing gently, and moved further in. With a graceful spreading of arms that seemed like wings, Judith reached herself into the water and was gone like a turtle. The slender, sweet-looking young god watched her for a moment, and then like an arrow put himself in the water beside her. Both movements had been so lucid, and the whole scene so moving and pure, that I felt I was on the edge of the only kind of life that mattered.

But I had the feeling that I was not the only watcher. Across from me the bushes seemed to stir, and I felt that someone was there, like myself surreptitiously peering out. In an instant the air had become polluted. I wanted to be away from it all, away from a presence that dirtied and destroyed. My curiosity had died in me. Turning hurriedly though still silently, I stumbled in the direction of the farm-house, the dogs with me.

It was only afterwards that I remembered how the hair of their backs had risen, and, also how, as I moved clumsily off, like a finger on my cheek I was touched again by the god-like sweetness of the two bathers in their crystal pool.

5

Purple, angry clouds came up thick and fast that afternoon. Over the white sheet of the vlei I could see their forerunners scudding along, quickly drawing the first curtains of fog behind them. And yet, standing as I was on the lawn, still caught in sunlight, I built round myself an ostrich shell of security. Nothing could spoil this world! The picture I had seen earlier that day of the two bathers could not be destroyed. But then, like a sly finger trailing down my back, I was reminded of that earlier sensation of a beast crawling in the undergrowth.

The stoep had become as dark as a cave. Thalia came out and stood beside me.

'The maids are lighting the lamps, and, do you know, it's not yet four. I hope this isn't going to mean day upon day of rain and fog. The company inside wouldn't take kindly to it.'

'They've all got in, have they?'

'Judith and Tony haven't got back yet from their picnic. I think a few others are still out. Monica's beginning to fret. She fusses over that girl. Judith — she's a rare creature, isn't she?'

'Yes.'

But already I was deep in thought. Where could they still be on an afternoon such as this? Certainly not in the pool. The mist had begun to come thickly, in waves, across the lawn.

I went inside with Thalia. Mrs. Hardwood was sitting comfortably beside the blazing log fire, working at a drawing. Eric was behind her doing the same. Monica had returned to her medical book. Samuel Smith was staring emptily at what seemed to be nothing at all.

'Ah, you've got in,' Thalia said to him. 'Where's your wife?'

'She'll be here shortly. She's in the rondawel.'

'I'm worried about Judith!' said Monica, looking up.

'Don't — let her take her time.'

'But look at the weather! And they've

been out since mid-morning.'

'It's exciting weather to be out in. But if they're not in soon, we'll send someone to look for them.'

Libby and Elsie had settled together in cat and dog-like affection in front of the fire. Soon the domestic scene seemed to be completed with Desmond bringing in the tea. The room was a golden pool as outside it steadily grew darker. The purple of the incoming clouds had changed to black-blue, visible through the sheets of scudding fog.

Thalia served tea, the pot steaming cheerfully in our midst. The large, sweet biscuits were good, too. Liquid amber melted down my throat, warming my chest and stomach as it came. All very comfortable. Yet *where* could they be?

Monica got up suddenly and went to stand at the window, her fingers drumming impatiently on the sill.

Just then Charmaine appeared.

'Why didn't someone call me?' she demanded petulantly. 'I've been terrified out in the rondawel.'

The remark seemed an odd one. Why

hadn't she come in? Why, on this particular day, should she stay in the rondawel, cowering in the face of the approaching storm?

Yet she seemed at heart a good-tempered creature, and she regained her equilibrium almost immediately.

'It looks good,' she said, with a pink bright hand taking her cup of tea, and then a biscuit. 'You two are still drawing are you, even though there's going to be an awful storm? Where are the others?' She looked quickly around her.

Monica half-turned from the window.

'We're terribly worried about them . . .'

It was one of the few occasions she had responded to Charmaine directly.

'Don't be such a fuss — you're a typical spinster,' replied the married lady brightly.

I could see that Monica had a strong reply ready, but she bit it off and turned back to the window. Charmaine continued chattering.

The room was becoming delightfully warm. In spite of a lingering feeling of unease I settled down to a book.

★   ★   ★

Then it hit us. There were no warning drops. Just a sheet of water, as though the sea of the heavens had cracked its ocean bed. It hit the windows which shuddered under its impact. It crashed down on the thatch.

For a moment I thought:

'Oh God! The place is collapsing.'

But the house had been strongly and carefully, if crudely, built, and the thatch was thick and weathered. Thalia looked thoughtfully at Monica beside the window. Then she went to the kitchen to see if any crises were developing in the servants' quarters.

I put down my book and went to stand beside Monica. The shoulder she half-turned on me was cold.

'Dear God!' she said out of the corner of her harddrawn mouth. I felt a deep pang of pity for her. She was so hard and so vulnerable, so brittle. I would almost have put my hand on hers, but I knew she'd shake it off angrily. She didn't want sympathy. Yet she needed it very much.

The lawn was under water now, a wide grey sheet machine-gunned by the incessant, hard rain. I felt the girl stiffening beside me. Someone had darted into the dubious shelter of a hedge — and then, as I watched, came out again, running for the house. Tony materialised as a quick, lithe spectre across the lawn.

He burst into the room, very much alive, shirt and shorts sodden, his legs and arms streaming, his hair plastered down like mud. He was panting, drawing quick, hard gasps of breath. For the moment he stood open-mouthed, like a fish that had been landed, gaping.

'Where's Judith?'

The words came from Monica with the effect of a riflecrack. There seemed to be a start in the room. I realised then how tense we had become.

Tony continued to gasp and gape, his eyes still large and glazed like those of a fish.

That insistent finger had started on my back once again. Angrily, I tried to shake it off. This vague, silly fear!

'Where is she?'

Again the words were fired at him.

'I don't know.' He gaped again in that stupid fish-like manner. 'I've . . . I've been looking for her . . . I couldn't find her . . . Hasn't she come in?'

'I wouldn't ask you if she was here, would I?'

There was ugly antagonism between them: not only anxiety, but the strong hand of jealousy had been laid on Monica. I perceived, with a sickening of heart, that at that moment, and perhaps before, she had learnt to hate the young man in front of her. What sort of a rival was he?

I felt sick again, not only for Tony and Judith, but for Monica, standing alone like a hard, frightened Medusa.

'My God, do you mean to say you've left her out there?'

He, in turn, was angry and frightened. 'What could I do? I couldn't find her. I thought she'd come back.'

'Look,' I said, suddenly trying to gather myself, all of us, sensibly together, 'this won't get us anywhere. Let Tony get himself dry. We'll then try to work out what happened.'

'Meanwhile she's out there!' exclaimed Monica bitterly, turning again to the window. But there had been a lull in the storm, and Tony, as if obeying orders, went to dry himself off.

Monica moved restlessly about the room, palpably trying to shake off her anger and her terrible fear.

'Do settle down!' said Charmaine, with growing irritation.

The tigress continued to stalk about the room. She was only subdued by Thalia coming in and persuading her towards the tea-table.

'We'll find out in a minute, Monica, and all will be well. You'll see.'

'I hope so,' said the girl miserably. Again I felt a quick, inexplicable pang of sorrow for her.

Tony, now towelled down and his skin gleaming ruddily, came back into the room.

'When last did you see her?' Thalia asked him.

'We had our picnic after we'd been bathing . . . ' He was still slightly breathless. 'I lay down to sleep. She said she was going off to bathe again — was going to try one of the smaller pools higher up. That's the last I saw of her.'

'Where did you look for her?' Thalia hurried on, trying to cover over the unpleasant suggestion of his last statement.

'When I went to sleep on that rock it was warm in the sun. When I woke up, everything had changed. I was shivering, the sky was purple, Judith wasn't there. It was so quiet, I felt uneasy. I collected our things together, and began going upstream, where she said she was going. I felt sure that if she had come down again to the house she would have woken me up on the way. The sky grew darker, and I passed pool after pool. I asked some of the farm workers who were on their way home. They hadn't seen her — one chap said he'd seen a ghost! I got right up to the main source of the stream. As I started coming down again, still looking, the storm burst. I couldn't see a thing then. I was sure she must have got home. But I felt it was so queer to leave me like that. I began to run as soon as I could see again.'

'She must have taken shelter somewhere,' said Thalia, 'and is waiting now
for the worst of the storm to pass.'

As if in answer to her desire, the storm
stopped, almost as suddenly as it had
begun. The silence was unnerving.

'We can go out now to look for her,'
said Monica at the window.

'Give her a short while to get back,'
said Thalia sensibly.

'By that time the storm will have
broken again.'

She seemed to be accusing us all of
some terrible plot to keep Judith out of
the house.

The rain didn't start again, and the
silence continued. But darkness began to
fall, and Thalia, with the lighting of the
lamps, decided we had waited long
enough. She questioned Desmond again,
and Samantha. They had seen nothing,
heard nothing, but, said Samantha,
someone had spoken about a ghost.
Thalia cut her short, despatched Desmond to the Braaks, and Samantha to the
native stad, to see if they could glean
information. Perhaps Judith had gone to

one of these as the nearest place of shelter.

'We'd better re-trace Tony's steps,' decided Thalia. 'I know this part of the country, and I'll lead the way up-stream. Tony had better come with me, and you Simon.'

'I'm coming too,' said Monica.

'That's all right. Perhaps you, Mrs. Hardwood, and Charmaine and Samuel, could mount the home front. Eric could come to us should Judith appear in the meantime. Strangely, I feel she's not too far away.'

We had torches and Thalia carried a storm lantern. The lights started bobbing out under the Jacaranda trees, up through the gate, on their way to the stream. Tiger had been brought with us, and Waif insisted on following as well. Monica was consumed by misery, but she concentrated on flashing her torch from bush to bush. Her life was not a sedate one, I could see that, even in the anxious darkness: she could become consumed by a range of apprehension. What was she expecting to find, what did she expect to be revealed? We had passed one of the heavily wooded areas where in the morning the cicadas had made their intolerable noise. It was very near to the pool where I had been a silent observer. Distressingly, Waif set up a howl, pouring anguished shrieks into the night. Tiger moved quickly, sniffing eagerly. She couldn't be as near as this.

'That horrible dog!' This from Monica in a voice charged with hatred.

'We'd better have a general look around,' said Thalia, flashing her light into the dense bush.

Tony had been silent throughout, and he went deeper than any of us, looking . . . Monica stood to one side, apparently uninterested, as if this was no place to begin our search. To her we were simply wasting time. Judith would surely have spoken or cried out had she hurt herself. We continued up-stream where Tony and Judith had bathed that morning. How beautiful it had been; what a terrible sequel this. But the pool still had beauty, because as we passed it the moon suddenly broke away from its steel rim of storm cloud, and the water was burnished beneath us, the rocks jutting out on the sides like majestic whales. Surely, in this world there could be no evil.

'Come on!' said Monica impatiently. Both Thalia and I had paused. Tony seemed to have forgotten that there was beauty, that there had been a morning, that life was going on. His movements had become mechanical, as though the end were in sight and perfectly predictable.

We struggled from pool to pool, our feet tangling in the long grass, the undergrowth, the ferns. The stream tinkled and gurgled on its silver way in a storm-crowded night. As we pushed up towards the source the rain began coming down again, first gently; then the drops became bigger, harder.

'Damn!' said Thalia. Monica had no words too strong for the wilfulness of nature.

We had now come into the upper kloof, and the banks stood darkly on either side of us, the thicker trees sheltering us from the storm. We all, I think, knew it was futile. Yet we *had* to go on searching.

'Perhaps she's back by now,' said Thalia. 'I think we should start cross country in case she slipped on one of the rocks or in the long grass, though I feel that some of the farm workers going home would have seen her. But we'd better try that route. If Eric looks for us he'll see the lights.'

It was still raining fiercely as we crossed the plateau of long grass, flashing our lights here, there, even up at the sky in a gesture of futility and prayer. Monica was getting beside herself. Something was building up, some long pentup rage, some resentment at the way in which life had used her. Tony was silently miserable. Thalia was marching ahead, determinedly, despite her anxiety her slender body swinging easily at the hips.

But the veld was empty and silent apart from the heavily spurting rain. We arrived back at the farm-house, bedraggled and praying for Judith to be waiting for us, comfortable beside the fire.

Eric came out to meet us. His enquiry

announced our disappointment. 'Any luck?'

I thought at that moment that Monica was going to tear him apart, she was so full of hatred.

'It's your fault,' she spat, turning on Tony.

He didn't reply. We went in silently.

Desmond was back from the Braaks — no, they hadn't seen her. Samantha was back from the stad — no, but there was this ghost.

'Stop that, Samantha!' exclaimed Thalia, uncharacteristically abrupt.

There was nothing to be done. We sat miserably in front of the fire, even Thalia seeming to have lost her direction, her sense of leadership. It was Mrs. Hardwood who made coffee, and sent it into us in big, steaming mugs. Desmond and Samantha were sent off for the night, but told to be on the ready should they be needed again.

We sat silently without Judith, who had become for us the world's desire.

'I'm sure she'll be here soon,' said Samuel Smith suddenly, ineffectually trying to rally the disconsolate room.

'Don't be a fool!' said Monica, who seemed to have given up hope.

'I'm going to ring the police now — this has gone on long enough,' Thalia announced. She went off to the telephone.

We could hear her tap-tap-tapping. It seemed like an echo of our own futility. Tap-tap-tap. Tap-tap-tap.

She came back.

'I'm sorry to tell you that the lines are down. That was a monster of a storm. I think we'd better try the Braaks' telephone, although I suspect it's pretty general, and that for the moment we're cut off.'

Eric and I toiled across the rise to the Valley of the Braaks, and knocked — it was perhaps nearly midnight — at their solid, ornate door.

Mr. Braak, clothed in voluminous striped pyjamas, and a shot-gun in hand, opened the door to us.

'What the hell, man!'

We had to explain quickly that Judith was still missing, and as we got across to the telephone as quickly as we could, we were joined by Mrs. Braak in a long, flowing nightgown, like a ghost on her wall to wall carpeting. She was full of enquiries.

The telephone was dead. We were beyond the reach of the world. She persisted in her enquiries, but I interrupted her.

'I think we'll have to drive to town. We must hurry.'

But it was at that moment standing with Mr. Braak and his shot-gun, and Mrs. Braak in her night-gown, in their unrealistically luxurious room, on their wall to wall carpeting, that nature gave its answer. A long, booming roar sounded down the valley.

'What's that?'

'You won't get to town, man,' said Mr. Braak. 'It's the river. It's coming down as it hasn't in ten years. The roads are all cut off, man, and'll be deep under water. We're cut off, man.'

The roar grew louder. I had seen the tawny monster of an enraged South African river before, a wall of water sweeping angrily down the valley. We were, indeed, cut off.

Disconsolately, silently, Eric and I went back to the homestead. Monica had gone to bed, having been forced to accept one of the potent tranquillisers Thalia insisted on keeping in stock despite the peacefulness of her farm. Charmaine had also gone to bed, complaining of a severe headache. The rest of us sat looking at one another. There was certainly not going to be sleep for us.

As we sat there staring vacantly, I was struck by an intuition so strong, that it became knowledge.

'We must go back.'

'Back where, Simon?' Thalia looked at me, her eyes ringed by blue. I was shocked to find how hopeless she had become. The curse of the valley had come true. That half-submerged story of her past life was back, and the dangerous beauty of the farm had been crucified into ugly, garish shapes.

'We must go back to where Waif started crying.'

'But you know he cries about everything. We searched that part, if you remember. It's so near the house that Judith could have got back if she'd been able to.'

Tony looked up, his face white and haggard.

'We must go back,' I repeated doggedly.

'I'll come with you,' Samuel said quietly.

'And I'd better come,' said Thalia. 'We must of course cover every possibility, however hopeless.'

In the end all that remained of the party decided to come, except Mrs. Hardwood. The rain had stopped as we went out once more with our lanterns and torches, a chinese expedition making its way slowly up the hill. Tiger and Waif were with us again. This time, unnervingly, Waif was wailing uncontrollably, running ahead obsessed with the surety I felt.

We reached the clump of thorn-trees. Waif jumped hysterically ahead. But it was Tiger who seemed so sure this time as he arrowed into the bush. With a prickling of our skins we heard his sharp, excited whine.

We struggled into the undergrowth, flashing our torches to where he stood over something. It was Judith, her body half-turned, her long blue-black hair trailing in a pool of water.

And then that thin red line. Her throat had been neatly cut.

6

What followed was a nightmare. We went through the motions of action like zombies. It was Samuel Smith, surprisingly strong, who lifted the body up, and said:

'We must get out of this.'

It would have been an insult to the dead to leave her lying there a moment longer.

'Oh my God,' said Thalia. That was the only other comment that was offered as we struggled home with our gruesome burden, Eric and I silently taking over from Samuel. Tony, it seemed, was beyond action. He stumbled back with us like an automaton.

The fear on Mrs. Hardwood's face stood out in the warm lanterns of the sitting-room.

'Get her to my room,' she said. 'I'll lay her out properly. I'm a trained nurse.'

We were guided by anyone who could

give us directions. As we turned, clumsy with our burden, Monica was in front of us standing in the doorway. The shock and horror, but, worse than this, the completeness of her despair, chilled us numb though we had already become used to shock. For some moments she could say nothing, her mouth working soundlessly like an imbecile's.

And then it came out, cold and hard.

'You murderers, all of you!'

Thalia started towards her.

'You murderer! You murderer! Getting her here to kill her!'

She was beginning to shriek, like a mad woman. It was Mrs. Hardwood who took action. She slapped her across the face.

Monica's hysterics ended, and she broke down into a pitiable, babbling object. Mrs. Hardwood was cold, purposeful.

'Put Judith in my room. I'll attend to Monica first.'

She took her off, firmly, by the arm. There was no resistance, the girl stumbling beside her, broken and bent-backed.

This time Tony carried the body, his

face as pale as river clay. I was disturbed by a horrible, ludicrous picture: a couple in love, he carrying his bride to the bridal chamber.

Thalia, practical once again, had gone off to summon Desmond from his bed. He would have to find the canoe, and paddle at least one of us across the water to try to reach the main road on the other side. After some minutes, he appeared in the sitting-room, his black skin gleaming, and yet an ugly ashen colour. He quite clearly was in a state of shock himself and kept on exclaiming:

'O, o, o, o . . . '

Eric and I walked heavy-footedly beside him, down the avenue now rutted with treacherous pools. The water got deeper as we drew nearer the vlei. We struggled in the chocolate darkness trying to follow the high contours of the land. The moon came out again, hateful and indifferent, but at least showing us our way. The concrete jetty had been built on the edge of the vlei, well above the level of the land, but there was water all around it now. We were up to our waists when finally we touched the cold brick and clawed our way over the edge. The canoe was there, filled with water but otherwise well to the side of the angrily flowing stream.

There would clearly be too many for this little boat, and so Eric stayed behind to await our arrival. God alone knew how long we would be before we found help, or at least the law.

Desmond paddled off, feeling his way across the night, touching uncertainly against the reeds and pushing himself off into the stream once more. The egrets had been roused by the storm and were winging like wild ghosts across the mad moon. We seemed for hours to thread our way in and out of reed clusters, getting caught by sudden streams, pulled away in odd directions, until Desmond felt the current again and cut across it. The rushing and fierce hissing was terrible, after the calm, placid water it had been.

At last this stage of the nightmare journey was over. We came under the bridge of the main road. Desmond put in at what remained of the bank, and we

clambered clumsily up, slipping danger-
ously as we pulled the canoe behind us.
We were now on the main road, but miles
away from anywhere. Would a car come?

One did appear ten minutes later,
veered towards us as it caught us in its
lights, and then dashed crazily off. We
must have looked an odd, terrible couple.
We were left in the silence of the road,
and help seemed a long way off. We were
in a mad world and there was no God, no
man, to help us.

'Should we try to find a farm-house?' I
broke the silence.

'Their telephones won't work, master.
The storm has come down all the kloofs.'

This seemed unanswerable as we
listened to the water whirling below us.

Then another car did come, and it did
stop. A couple on the way from Sabie to
White River, intending to get to the
nearest gate of the Game Reserve by the
first light of morning. A mad scheme, but
everything seemed beyond credence that
night. Desmond waited at the bridge with
the boat as I went off with them. They
questioned me eagerly, but I tried not to

tell them anything beyond hinting at a great crisis occasioned by the sudden flood.

The police station, luckily, was open, and I insisted on being dropped and left. I didn't want the story in and out of the game parks, up and down the Eastern Transvaal, before I could help it.

A young constable was on duty, bewildered by what I told him, but prompt in getting through to the senior sergeant on call. Within minutes Sergeant Combrink was with us, a burly, rough-faced man. He questioned me gruffly. In trying to answer him I realised something that the shock of Judith's death had removed from my mind, from all our minds, it seemed, despite Monica's hysterical words. A murderer was loose amongst us, was probably on the farm, sitting normally with normal people.

He was coming with me. Rapidly he made his plans, and the young constable drove us to where Desmond waited. He set off with Desmond. Eric would be at the other end to take him further. The constable waited with me until Desmond returned, and I realised this wasn't simply for company and comfort's sake. I, too, was under suspicion, and must not be allowed to slip away towards the border. Silently, sitting on the desolate bridge, I began to question myself, my actions, my motives, and it seemed that I wasn't sane after all. These premonitions I had had. Were they not simply the building up of a nervous excitement over which I had no control? I tried to shake myself back into normality. The inquisitive conversation of the young constable didn't help me, and I was relieved when, finally, as dawn began to break so splendidly, I heard the canoe returning.

The flooded valley was a paradise of gold and topaz as we paddled back into the storm waters. Everything seemed sharp, abundant, fiery with life. I have seldom seen anything more beautiful. The song-birds, the thrushes, sang to the morning, the green and yellow bokmaki-eries were on the wing, the rock pigeons hovered overhead. A paradise.

And yet a body waited for us. The body of a lovely young girl, with blue-black hair

— her throat expertly cut.

The wonder of it somehow made it more difficult for me to control my nerves. It was a paradise into which a beast had been let loose. I was glad when we reached the jetty. I was even glad to be stumbling waist deep in the mud and slush towards the avenue, where the wood owls were hooting incongruously in the splendour of a bright morning.

The scene that greeted me as I came in was as unreal as anything else. Sergeant Combrink was sitting to one side with Thalia, questioning her intently. She was strained, and for the first time seemed artificial, exotic in her setting, with her clear, English voice. The sergeant seemed normal, as though he belonged to her farm-house. The guests, sitting silently to one side, seemed no longer an interesting, lively group, but a bunch of misfits, all of them glum, Monica glassy-eyed, Tony like a shady ghost of the young god he had been the day before. For a moment his beauty seemed sordid, and I felt a pin-prick of resentment.

Things weren't helped by the appearance of the Braaks, and they had to learn the truth.

'One of the boys says he's seen someone in the valley, someone searching for murder.'

'What's this?' Sergeant Combrink looked up sharply. Mrs. Braak could really tell him very little. Besides, the servants who had spoken of the ghost were on the other side of the valley, in the native stad now cut off by the floods.

'Man, this is terrible! It's never happened here before,' said Mr. Braak, looking accusingly at Monica. 'There's been no scandal here, man, except that business about your brother.'

'That's nothing to do with this,' Thalia said quickly, but it seemed that the past was indeed thumbing itself into the terrible present.

After a while Sergeant Combrink managed to get the Braaks to go back home. Mr. Braak had an ominous parting shot:

'Do you realise, man, that there's only these two houses in this part of the valley? We've been cut off by the floods, man, we're alone. Perhaps if we have to get away we can get through the hills on the other side of The Grapevine.'

'Impossible,' said Combrink curtly. 'The Hendriks River has really come down in flood, and it's worse than this.'

'Oh my Lord,' said Mrs. Braak. 'We've really had it, then.'

Later on, after a few more general questions, Combrink sent us to our rondawels, while he questioned each of us separately. But, whenever we could, we all listened to the questioning on the stoep. We learned some very interesting things.

Monica, still stunned, was one of the first to be questioned, kindly, I thought, by the rough-voiced man. For the most part her answers were inaudible. But at one stage, with a sudden excitement, her voice was raised and querulous.

'She said she was on to something!'

'What do you think she meant by that, doctor?'

'She had found out something relating to the history of this area, and it affected someone, I think — here.'

Her voice which had been listless until

then was touched by a sudden dread.

'Something important enough to make someone kill her, do you think?'

His questioning was purposely even.

She hesitated for a moment.

'Yes, I think so.'

'Did she explain what she meant by 'here'? In this house? In the valley?'

Again she hesitated and the voice began to tail off into listlessness.

'I'm not sure . . . '

He let her go after that. Mrs. Hardwood gave her an injection of some kind, for she was in a quietly frantic state.

It was strange about Mrs. Hardwood. She had never mentioned being a nurse. Yet it seemed that she was a highly trained one, and a highly regarded one, before something happened.

'What was it that happened?' I heard her being questioned.

Her flat voice was remarkably clear. Her answer provided something of a jolt.

'I took the law into my own hands.'

'In what way? Did you do something criminal?'

'Not in my opinion.'

It seemed that she had performed an emergency operation, technically easy but a vital one, when the surgeon could not be found. He was located the next day recovering from a drunken binge. He was the only surgeon in the district, the only competent one.

'I didn't trust the other doctors in the district. They were inexperienced.'

'You trusted yourself?'

'I had to — I thought so. I could have been a doctor.'

The patient had lived and flourished. Mrs. Hardwood had been spared the worst vengeance of the courts. She had been found guilty and fined, and dismissed as a nurse. The district had lost their greatest medical benefactor. She, in turn, had tried to lose herself in Johannesburg.

'I had lived for my profession.'

The story was astounding. I remembered my fanciful idea about each person on the farm being a suit-case of secrets. How little we knew each other. Judith and her husband. Thalia's brother. The ghost of the valley.

Mrs. Hardwood had laid the body decently out on her bed. After having carefully examined it, and later having related it to the place where it was found, Sergeant Combrink had to make arrangements for the post-mortem and funeral. Desmond had been despatched once more across the flood waters, a launch of sorts had been found by the local police, and late in the afternoon the men on the farm had to assist Judith's uneasy passage across the mud.

Sergeant Combrink returned. He slept that night in the sitting-room. No one sat up. We all went early to our rondawels, and at various times until eleven o'clock I heard him moving from rondawel to rondawel, questioning people in a deep undertone.

I was also questioned in the light of the gas lamp, but I couldn't tell him anything substantial. Premonitions, fingers down one's back, the beast in the undergrowth — all that had become ludicrous because the unthinkable had happened. I didn't feel my premonitions were justified. I felt simply that they had become petty. And so I held my tongue about them. Yet when I looked up I saw his green eyes on my face, quietly puzzled.

The night was hot.

★　★　★

The next morning the sun was up again in a golden blaze. Desmond reported early that the road was passable, a hazardous, muddy route, but passable.

The funeral was to be that afternoon. We set out in two cars: all of us, with the exception of Charmaine, who had declared herself not up to a journey, or a funeral. But she was not going to stay alone in 'that place'; she had formed a sudden friendship with Mrs. Braak and would be spending the afternoon at The Grapevine. She would, I think, like to have been well away from Bloedplaas, but Sergeant Combrink had made it clear that none of us was to leave.

Monica, a waxen image of a woman, travelled this time with Eric, Thalia and Mrs. Hardwood in the first car. She could not bear to be anywhere near Tony, who sat beside me. Samuel shared the back seat with Sergeant Combrink.

It was a grim little ceremony. A parson, summoned for the occasion, hurried pedantically through the ceremony. There were a great many curious onlookers, but only the eight mourners who had come from the farm. Or, no, there were nine. A burly, dark man had attached himself to the party, had brought a wreath. He didn't speak to any of us, except when we were about to leave. I became aware of Combrink standing beside him, listening courteously. They were earnest words they exchanged. I saw the sergeant make some notes in the little book he always carried with him.

It was a sultry day, but as we left the cemetery the clouds gathered once again like a purple bruise against the sky.

'Do you know who that was?' said Combrink as we started on the journey back. He didn't seem reluctant to give information.

I waited for his next statement. In fact no one spoke.

'That was Mrs. Price's husband.' He

paused for a moment before he qualified the statement. 'Or, shall I say, her ex-husband.'

Tony drew in his breath sharply beside me. I picked up his face in the mirror. It was ashen, and slightly contorted, the mouth beginning a grimace of pain. What was it — guilt, jealousy, love, grief? In the mirror I saw other eyes were looking interestedly at him: Samuel's suddenly quite sharp behind their glasses; and the bolder look of Combrink. There would be further interrogation, I could see. Not that he was a detective of the urbane British school. He pursued his homespun, dogged course.

'But what did he want?' I at least had the presence of mind to ask.

'To mourn for his wife. But, also, to give information.'

We were all listening, breaths drawn in.

'I got the idea, you know, that he didn't really want to give information — ' Again the almost imperceptible pause. 'But that he was frightened.'

'But of what?'

114

'What his wife was frightened of. She had reason to be, didn't she?'

'But how did he happen to be on the spot, as it were?'

I pressed on with my own questioning while I had the opportunity.

'For years now, from what I could gather, he'd been following up his own investigation in this part of the world. It's this investigation that came between them, that led to the first break in their marriage. This much I could gather. The rest is still a mystery.'

'But don't you have any idea why he spoke to you? Surely not simply because he was frightened, had a vague fear?'

'No, he had something very specific to give me. Mrs. Price wrote to him, the day before her death. She had something to tell him.'

'What was it, sergeant?'

'That I don't know, but I have something better than what he could have told me.' Again the imperceptible pause. He was slightly enjoying his moments of drama. 'I have the letter itself.'

This time it was not a pause. There was

a deathly hush. Were we near to the answer? The car purred loudly as we drove into the purple sky.

He said almost casually:

'I haven't read it yet.'

No one questioned him any further. The heavens gathered over us, and we knew that the storm was about to burst again, even more violent than before. We should perhaps have considered turning back, but no one even suggested it. We drove on, to the isolation of an island, to whatever it was that was waiting for us.

I swung on to the farm road, spearing its way into the deep hills. Deeper than blood.

We had only just crossed the dubious mud patches of the Bloedplaas road, when the storm burst violently. We were once more prisoners, we and the unknown killer.

7

We had to run for the house, the big drops hitting us like diamonds. A curtain of water swept across the scenery.

We were all drenched when we arrived on the stoep. The others had come before the rain had started, and were having tea. Charmaine, apparently, was still with the Braaks.

Thalia had already been at work.

'You're drenched,' she said to Sergeant Combrink. 'And you can't go back to the sitting-room to sleep. I've moved you into my bedroom — I'm going to share a rondawel with Monica, with Dr. Thurle.'

The big man for once was embarrassed.

'No, you shouldn't have done that, Miss du Mont. What about Dr. Thurle — won't she mind?'

Monica didn't seem to be capable of minding anything. She remained in her glassy state. She wasn't cold, just glassy, dead, without hope — I realised, with a stab of compassion, how much this superior woman had cared for her companion. She and Tony were the two people who didn't seem to be able to recover from their shock. Yet Tony had for her become a sworn enemy. She was cut off from everyone, except Thalia and, possibly, Mrs. Hardwood, who, very strangely, on that weirdly lighted stoep, had begun drawing an oak-tree.

She seemed to have been the first to find her way to recovery, as though she had seen danger and suffering many times before. And we had thought her such a helpless old lady, someone who was no doubt game, but who needed protection from the shocks of the world.

Combrink looked at her for a moment, speculatively, before he went with Thalia to inspect his room.

I wanted to talk to Monica, but had nothing to say to her. I, too, went off to change. Samuel and Tony had already disappeared to do the same.

When I came back to the stoep Combrink and Thalia had not yet appeared. Then I saw them in the sitting-room, their faces close together, talking like conspirators. A shadow was on Thalia's face, and it seemed for a moment that the past was reaching across the rain-sodden lawn, across the stoep, into the sitting-room. What could the connection be? For I felt now there *must* be a connection.

'How are you feeling?' I said to Monica, stilted, boyishly inadequate.

She didn't answer, just sat staring into the rain. I sat beside her, though I felt that my presence was most unwelcome.

'I wonder if you shouldn't get away. This has probably been too much for you.'

She spoke out of the side of her mouth, not looking at me.

'Do you think I'm going to let this beast escape?'

It came with something of a shock to hear the fanciful term of my premonitions — 'beast' — translated so flatly. It seemed to make the danger worse. The premonition had become a tangible thing; an uneasy spirit had become an ugly, crawling object.

Her next statement shocked me.

'But not quite a beast. It knows, for example, how to cut throats competently — the work of a surgeon.'

I was bewildered, and didn't know how to answer her.

'Or of a highly trained nurse, who could have been a doctor?'

The words came from Mrs. Hardwood, who was looking up angrily over her drawing, her face flushed.

We couldn't deny we hadn't heard about her. No one attempted an answer.

'I see you know the disgraceful story. It's impossible to escape one's past, isn't it? Here I thought was I a nice, tree-drawing old lady — and I'm a criminal caught out. I feel that this is a prison.'

She stared at the bars of rain. Her face showed not so much hatred, as pure frustration at the way life had used her. She had so much competence to bring; she had saved life — and the world of conventions brought her dismissal, social imprisonment.

It seemed as though she were answering me.

'I tried to find escape in drawing trees. I'll never draw people,' she said, looking belligerently at Tony, who had now appeared.

She had liked Eric's sketches after her first surprise, but now could not like them. She could not bear the vision of the naked, and therefore tainted, humanity the boy represented.

She turned back to her drawing.

Monica had stared on, as if untouched. Yet knowledge crinkled along the edges of her eyes. It was knowledge, self-knowledge; she had begun to learn something about herself.

It was Eric who made the next move in this curious charade. He got up and went to sit next to Mrs. Hardwood.

'Look here, Mrs. H,' he said. 'I don't give a damn whether you were responsible for an illegal operation or not. That was a long time ago, wasn't it? I bet you've looked at yourself a great deal since then. We don't have the right to go on examining you. What matters to me are your drawings, which I think are fine things. I like you, too. You're filled with the need for life, whether it be operations or drawings.'

It was a rough speech, roughly delivered. But it was a good one, and Mrs. Hardwood looked up at Eric, her stiff face softening in the grey light.

'Thank you — Eric. You're right: I'll go on, because — ' and she was suddenly awkward, 'because I still believe in life.'

She looked at Tony now, and I realised she was a remarkable person, not at all set in her ways, not as set as so many young, apparently enterprising, go-getters.

I saw, too, that Monica had turned her gaze from the rain, and was looking at her in another new dawning of knowledge. Ours was not only, it seemed, a mystery of violence and murder, but a mystery of personality: people running away from themselves, looking for themselves, coming through, going under.

I was touched by an almost petty resentment that Eric had made the first move, because I knew that Mrs. Hardwood had also liked me. But I had, of course, done my duty in trying to approach Monica, apparently without success.

But at least I was needed elsewhere, for just then Sergeant Combrink came to the sitting-room door.

'I wonder if you would join us, Mr. Digby?'

Thalia was sitting quietly in her comfortable chair, but I could see that she had been shaken.

She managed to smile at me.

'This hasn't been quite the holiday you or I envisaged, Simon,' she remarked. 'I had my illusions. I thought I could build an exquisite cocoon, wrap away the past with what I thought were my silken, competent threads. From what Sergeant Combrink tells me the past won't keep to its place, and perhaps I'm responsible . . . '

'That's rubbish,' said the sergeant pithily. 'All that I'm saying is that we must look into rumours because it seems to me there's a background to all this. The letter seems to show it.'

'And how the pieces fit together we just can't tell. Perhaps they're not related, the past and this thing . . . '

'But the indications suggest they are.'

He turned to me.

'I'd better explain why we've got you here, sir. Now, to begin with, a chap must know himself a bit. I'm landed in this, and I'm not all that good at this sort of case. We were getting the Murder Squad into this from Johannesburg to take over, but it's my guess they won't get here for several days. Not with a storm like this — I think the valley is going to be flooded for a long time. We'd better face it, we're shut off. And if the experts can't get here I must have the advice of someone who knows the place, and as a journalist — a good journalist I think Miss du Mont said — you can see into things, into,' he hesitated, on the edge of what seemed pretentious terms, 'can see into human motive, and behind words . . . Also, of course, there's your great knowledge of the area.'

He hurried on.

'But there's another reason too, Mr. Digby. I don't want to sound melodramatic: but some other man here must know what's going on.' Again there was that pause. 'Must know ... in case something happens — to me. Because, you see, I think there's a character here who'll stop at nothing if someone seems to be getting on to something ... That's my guess. And another guess is that you're a bloke who can be trusted. I must play my cards somewhere, even in the dark.'

I wondered whether I could indeed be trusted. I felt unsure of my qualities, and in me the faint coward stirred. If I was to be burdened with knowledge, surely there was danger for me too. The sergeant took up my thoughts.

'And I don't think you're the kind of bloke who'll run away from danger.'

'And because of this, my sweet,' Thalia interrupted, 'I'll have to tell you my own sordid story, describe the cross you've guessed at. Because strange things have gone on on this farm, and are still going on.'

'But the first thing is the letter,' the sergeant interrupted. 'I've shown it to Miss du Mont. It's because of it that I've got her story from her.'

He put his big hand on the table and picked up the note, handing it to me.

'Here it is. Read it, Mr. Digby.'

'Dear Bert' it began.

'Bert?'

'That's her husband. Mrs. Price's ex-husband.'

Bloedplaas.

Dear Bert,

I may need your help, after all. When we parted I swore I'd never appeal to you again, not for anything. Your obsessions seemed more important than our life together.

And now I must eat a little humble pie and say that I think that you were partly right. Not that your obsession was right. That was wrong — and I've seen other obsessions, here, that have made me feel this even more. I'd better explain where I am, and what I'm trying to say.

I'm on Thalia du Mont's farm, Bloedplaas. I came here with Monica Thurle. I didn't really come to snoop. I came for what I thought would be a

126

perfect holiday. There are a great many perfections here, let me tell you that straight away: Thalia du Mont, for one thing; the beautiful farm, for another; some of the guests, for a third. But I thought, too, that being so near the gold-bearing parts I would just idly 'investigate' a few things I'd never understood. I think it's taken me too far, perhaps, and — I'm frightened, not too much yet, but fear is beginning. I must try to tell you something of what I know — not all, though, because I have no right to point fingers at people when I'm not sure.

I'm telling you this because you with your background knowledge of this part of the world may be able to help me. I'd like to say again that I was wrong, Bert, somewhere, and that I need your help.

You and your stories of the lost gold of Pilgrim's Rest! The way you had to chase off on every idiot's trail, after every crazy rumour, and leave me to my own devices. I just couldn't bear it after a while! But I don't want this to turn into a personal bleat. There may not be time for that. I want to see you; I want to tell you more; I want to get to the bottom of 'it'.

I came here, as I say, with no deliberate intention of following your trail. But I started looking again at Simon Digby's books — he's a house guest here, incidentally. Thalia du Mont showed me a few more books, and in one I came across a document (it had clearly been left there unintentionally many years before — the paper was somewhat brown, the ink a bit faded). I shouldn't have read it, but my curiosity had become more than academic. To put it in a nut-shell: the gold minted in the old South African Republic at the President's wish, *did* exist, and it *didn't* leave South Africa, it didn't cross the border. It was, in fact (at the time of writing, certainly), still very much in the Eastern Transvaal. A location was given. I've got this paper in my handbag.

I was about to turn it all into an adventure story, share it with my co-guests, when I found something else in one of Thalia's books that made me apprehensive, and then, stupidly I suppose, made me frightened. I can't quite understand it. I haven't said anything yet to anyone, not to Monica, not to Thalia. Yet I must have given something away somewhere, and, I'm frightened my dear, and yet I want your greedy dreams to come true. Oh Bert — those lost years! I can't bear to think of you wasting your life. You must have gone about your search very quietly because I don't think even Simon Digby knows about you.

But come quickly, I'm frightened. I want the story to have a conclusion. Or I must leave. If you say you'll come, I'll be here for another week.

Judith.

I put the letter down. So many questions. The trail of gold had led into this quiet valley, this lovely rural area. Judith had paid the price. But surely she had not died simply for a treasure — this would be to flatten a story that was much more intense, much more beastly.

'What do you make of it?'

'There's so much to be unravelled . . . To answer the easiest question first:

no, I had no idea of Bert Price and his activities. He must indeed have gone about his work quietly, because I have, of course, heard a great deal about the President's millions.'

'Where do you think they are?'

'As far as I knew — until this moment — they simply didn't exist. The figure, the amount of money, was legendary, but I thought it was too immense even for this legendary area.'

I turned then to Thalia.

'But I don't understand. How do you come into this?'

'The document in the book, dear boy. Someone must have put it there.'

'But who? It seems incredible.'

'Not so incredible when you know my story. Bert Price wasn't the only one with an obsession about the President's millions.'

'But who could have put it there?'

'The answer seems simple to me: my father — or my brother. And I bet you those notes are in one of their handwritings.'

'Can't you tell?'

'No, dear. Judith's document, as she calls it, has disappeared.'

'And she had to pay the price for possessing it?'

Thalia hesitated.

'Not entirely, I think. You remember there was something else she found in one of those books. She probably had to pay the price — for that.'

'But I'm bewildered.'

'So am I, but a mental twinge tells me I'm right.'

'And this is one of the things I want you to help me with, sir,' Sergeant Combrink interrupted. 'I want you and Miss du Mont to help me with those books — to go through each one of them with me. You have the knowledge to detect any clues. I don't know whether Miss du Mont told you: she found Mrs. Price had collected about forty books and magazines in her room, most of them old, rotten with dust.'

'Judith had begged to see all I had. She apparently went through them at night when she and Monica were back in their rondawel.'

'But what are we looking for?'

'If we knew that, sir,' said Sergeant Combrink patiently, 'we might have the answer to the mystery.'

'But how do we know that this second thing, this clue, hasn't been removed?'

'We just don't know, sir, but still we must look. I don't like saying it, but — another life may be at stake, and we're shut off in this valley.'

'This terrible valley,' Thalia echoed him.

'This wonderful valley, Miss du Mont. We can't help what human beings do to it. If they make something ugly we've got to try to stop them. That's what life's about, isn't it?'

He was slightly side-tracked as he enunciated his rough philosophy, and in the process became more human.

'There are a lot of terrible things said about the police in this country, and a lot of those things are true, worse luck! But I want to help make it a little better. In my own way I'm also a dedicated man, you see.'

His voice trailed off. I liked him. In

some ways we had been lucky in the policeman the floods had brought us.

'But enough of that stuff! We'd better start getting down to things.'

'I think, sergeant,' said Thalia, 'I'll tell Mr. Digby my own sad tale later on. You know it, and it'll save time to go on to other things that we haven't touched on together.'

'I think, too,' he said, 'that we'll do the books at night: each take some to their bedroom, and comb through them. What we'd better do now is to try to get the human picture in this valley straight — see how many people we think there are here, and what we have to look out for. God knows, if the rain keeps on, we may have to live with each other for quite a time. I have an idea that not even the police launch, such as it is, is going to keep us in touch . . . Just listen to that rain.'

The storm crashed around us, and there were faint booming noises as the torrent swept into the valley.

'I think we're on our own,' he said flatly.

To me, despite his laconic tone, it was like the voice of doom. We were on our own in the valley, with someone who was quite clearly an expert killer.

'How do we go on, sergeant?' Thalia asked.

'We'd better make a note of everyone we know to be in the valley. There can't be very many, because there are only two farm-houses here. All the labourers and most of the domestic staff live in the native stad, and that's been cut off by the flood.'

'Yes, it should be easy to name all the people here, unless — unless there's someone else on the farms that we can't account for.'

It was uncanny, for it was as though after she had said it, I felt someone creeping in the darkness, in the rain, watching us.

Combrink was more matter-of-fact.

'Well that we don't know. We'd better for the moment go on with what we do know.'

'Let's start with the people in this house. You and Mr. Digby here.' He glanced out onto the stoep. 'Mr. Shackleton, Mr. Reade, Miss Thurle, Mrs. Hardwood — ' Again an imperceptible pause, 'Mr. Smith.' Now there was no pause. 'But where's Mrs. Smith?'

'Oh, my god!' said Thalia. 'She's still at the Braaks. I'd better send Desmond to see what's happened to her.'

'Mr. Smith hasn't enquired about her — strange,' said the sergeant.

'I'm afraid he's not a man of great initiative at any time,' Thalia replied. 'In this case, I suppose I'd better take the lead.'

She hurried off to speak to Desmond, and we waited silently until her return.

'Well that's the guests accounted for,' said the sergeant, when she sat down again. 'What about the domestic servants?'

'There are only two here at present, Desmond and Samantha. The rest are in the stad.'

'You know,' the sergeant mused, 'I don't think this was an African witch-doctor sort of crime, or anything like that. Not savage enough. Too expert — too sophisticated. There seem to be so many other motives. They may not, of course, be the motives — there may be jealousy. There may not even be a motive. If that is so . . ' He paused in his slow, characteristic manner. 'If that is so, then, I'm afraid, we have to reckon with a homicidal maniac.'

A few seconds ticked by as we sat blankly, the flames of the hurricane lamps throwing vivid shadows against the walls, and across the stoep outside.

He became matter-of-fact once again.

'Let's go on with the business in hand. Your farm is accounted for. Now, the Braaks — any children, any guests?'

'The children, two of them, are at boarding-school. I know they haven't any house guests at the moment — Mrs. Braak is very busy making preserves.'

It sounded a little lame, this domestic occupation, and a little weird with the lights flickering, and the floods and rain crashing outside.

'What domestic servants?'

'She has a great many, but she can't bear to have them around the house at night she says. They all go off to the stad, except a girl, Rinka, who's always with her. I'm almost sure there are no other servants on this side of the valley.'

'We can check on that afterwards. I think, if you don't mind, we'll start looking at some of the characters we have with us, and see what we know about them.'

Just then Desmond came in. Charmaine was still at the Braaks and said she wouldn't be coming back that evening because of the rain and the murderer. Perhaps everything would be more normal the next morning. Then she would come, and perhaps leave immediately.

'She's got hopes!' the sergeant remarked laconically.

Thalia went out to the stoep. We heard her giving Samuel Smith the news. He received it stoically enough, but I couldn't help thinking how consistently disappointing Charmaine must be as a wife. At a time when, for all his quietness and acceptance, he perhaps needed her company most, she left him to himself in the rondawel.

Combrink continued his narration when Thalia came back.

'I've already looked at a few of the people here,' he said. 'Isn't it queer how we all manage to have a few skeletons tucked away. Take Mrs. Hardwood, for example — who will have guessed it of a quiet old dame, almost straight out of Dickens, except of course for her being in the veld.'

I looked at him curiously. This was certainly not the type of ultra-philistine we were led to expect in our policemen.

'But I like the old girl. She's got what I would call guts, savvy — she's shrewd, yet she'll do something courageous, or outrageous, or gentle and kind, if she feels it's right.'

He turned again to Thalia.

'But I want to ask you about someone in particular now. This man Braak. He's very rich, isn't he?'

'Very, almost fabulously so.'

'And he's made it all from farming?'

'No . . . ' Thalia hesitated. 'I don't think so. He's been involved in various enterprises — this was even more the case

138

in my parents' time. He was always successful. They were seldom so.'

'This is why I ask, Miss du Mont: I've heard this name mentioned more than once in the district in connection with this gold recovery scheme, and if I remember correctly, he made quite a lot of money out of gold.'

'I can't really say,' said Thalia. 'These schemes are so intricate.' Then she looked darkly at us both. 'He and my brother were found talking together more often than we liked.'

'And *he* was interested in gold, wasn't he?'

'They all were, then,' she said bitterly. 'All of them were. My father included. But that wasn't gold recovery . . . ' Her wry humour asserted itself for a moment. 'At least not as we understand the term today.'

'No, but it had quite a bit to do with the lost millions hadn't it?'

'Oh yes. I'll explain this to you later, Simon, if you're wondering what it's about. Sergeant, shouldn't I begin getting supper?'

'Please, Miss du Mont. I'd almost forgotten how little we've eaten today.'

Most people ate well, making clear that even in the middle of horror there was such a thing as survival. Only Monica didn't eat. She chewed a crust, and then silently sipped the cold white wine Thalia had served. Most of us had quite a lot of wine, and despite our unease, began to show signs of fatigue and sleepiness. One thing was curious. No one seemed to suspect or want to accuse the other, as one is led to believe in these cases. It seemed that to all of us the beast was outside. My suspicion had focused itself almost comfortably when Sergeant Combrink turned to Thalia again.

'Mr. Braak knows this valley well, doesn't he?'

'Like the back of his hand.'

Poor Charmaine. I wonder whether she knew what she had let herself in for. She thought she was escaping danger, and it was possible that she was running straight into the lion's jaws. I looked at Samuel. He didn't seem to have seen the implication, and then I realised how little interest he had in his wife. That humouring of her was like playing with a wilful child.

The sergeant didn't seem much like questions after supper, and after we had sorted Judith's books into three equal piles, he took himself off to bed, with a grunted goodnight. He was clearly absorbed in his own thoughts.

At last Thalia and I were alone. Without preamble she began.

'This is the story, my dear. The appearance of that man, Bert Price, has brought most of it back to me. I'm not going to relate all the sordid details, but please don't put what I do tell you into one of your books. I don't want to be reminded of it forever. It's all too close to me.'

I should perhaps state that Thalia did finally consent to my telling this story — perhaps because of the interesting circumstances in which we were to find ourselves a little later in life.

'As you know, my parents bought this farm over fifty years ago. They didn't really want to make money from farming;

my mother had a considerable inherit-
ance. They wanted to keep it going
because it seemed, to them too, the most
beautiful place on earth.

'But my father was obsessed by one
thing in this area — the lost millions of
the President. He was a gentle, generous
man but it was an obsession nevertheless . . . ' Her voice became quieter. 'An
obsession he shared with a very different
kind of person — my brother.'

She looked at the moths circling one of
the lanterns, her eyes blinking with the
memory.

'André was the proverbial ne'er-do-
well. He wasn't stupid by any means,
but he just couldn't settle down to a
job. He tried being an accountant, a
doctor, the manager of a grocery store
even. He wasn't bad at any of them, I
believe, but wanted something more
than trust, or even authority, in his
hands. I can only call it — power. He
got into trouble — I don't think it's
important for the moment what that
was — and before I came back he was
here with my parents. He wasn't

interested in helping run the farm. Oh dear me no. But he was interested in the President's gold. He went through all my father's maps and notes, until finally the old man, shocked by his indolence, by his greed, by something less tangible, more vicious, wouldn't tell him anything more.

'Something occurred to make them hate each other. I still don't know what it was, but I can guess. I've always been a little over-dramatic in the good tradition of journalism, but if my guess was right . . . ' She suddenly broke off, and then began again. 'At the time even I thought it was too wild, too absurd, but I feel more and more that I may have been right. If I was right, it was momentous.'

'What was it?'

'Simon, I think my father found the President's millions.'

The night seemed to gather darkly about us. There was a sudden scudding of the flame.

A window swung open.

★ ★ ★

143

Perhaps it was the wind, for there was nothing there when, tremblingly, I went to shut it.

'What is it?' said Thalia from where she sat.

'Nothing — it seems.'

She shivered. Her voice wasn't really light as she tossed off the next remark:

'The ghost of the valley, no doubt!'

'Where were we?' she continued as I sat down again. 'Ah yes, my father and the President's millions. I haven't any proof, mind you, of what I'm telling you. You'll just have to accept it as my intuition. This was about six months before I came back to the farm. But from my mother I gathered that André and my father began to quarrel violently. André sensed that my father had at last come on to something big, but the old man remained tight-lipped, even to my mother.

'And now the plot begins to thicken. About three months before I came back to the farm — and this partly induced me to return — André disappeared suddenly.'

'But why?'

'Someone else had come to learn my

father's secret. This was a farm servant, David, whom my father trusted probably more than he did anyone else. For some years he had been like a manservant, a bodyguard, to him, and he took him with him on his expeditions, leaving my mother and André waiting gloomily at home. Then one day — oh my God! That has to come back!'

She had caught her breath sharply, and was beginning to pant a little.

'Don't tell me if you don't want to, Thalia. I have no right to pry into your secrets.'

'I must tell you. Someone must know, apart from Sergeant Combrink. He knew part of the story, incidentally. Of course several people in the district know about it. The police have it on record as one of their unsolved crimes.'

I knew I did want to know, urgently.

'One day David was found with his throat cut. André disappeared and has never been seen since. He lost himself entirely in the wide world. At least — I *think* he has never been seen again. A body was found at Lourenço Marques very much like his. It was identified by my father, who made that long trip on his own. Yet he could have been wrong.'

The gusty night brought on an uncontrollable bout of shivering, but she managed to steady herself.

'There was, of course, nothing to pin the crime onto my brother, except the coincidence of his disappearance. For some time the police thought it could have been a sort of ritual murder but, then again, it was too — neat. And I wonder whether André could have achieved so tidy a murder; he was clumsy and hot-headed as I remember him.'

She paused, taking breath.

'Now we come to the time of my return, with my brother safely out of the way, and the fortune mine. Yet, if there was a fortune, it was never mentioned. My brother could, possibly, have got the plans from David, and disappeared money and all. A wealthy man seems to have so many ways of achieving anonymity.'

'The body at Lourenço Marques. Did you find out anything about it?'

'I can see the drift of your questions, my sweet. It was smartly clothed. The body of a wealthy man — the body of a wealthy man who has never been identified, except by my father. It seems that if the ghost of the valley *is* my brother, it could be a ghost indeed.

'But to come back to the time of my return. The year passed tranquilly enough, except for this shadow hanging over us. Tranquil, that is, until two nights before my parents' death. They had become curiously restless, and the following day, on some silly pretext, they sent me to town to spend the night with friends. I should have stuck it out, but it seemed so important to them that I should go.

'Desmond tells me that they had a visitor that night. I had to worm it out of him. He didn't see who it was, simply a shadow against a white wall, a low murmur in the night.

'I returned the next day. They were to go and see a neighbour that night, and, as you know, they never got there. The car, inexplicably, swerved over the bridge and they were drowned in the Aardstroom which was flowing strongly then — that's where you and Desmond must have put to the evening you went for the police.'

'And you think your brother has come back?'

'If he has he's skulking in the valley, and, incidentally, keeping himself hidden very well. Yet someone surely would have identified him had they seen a strange, uninvited visitor.'

'This man, Bert Price, Judith's husband. His interests seem to have coincided so closely with those of your father and brother. Could your brother not have changed his name, married Judith — and when he got her warning, decided she had to be removed? I know it sounds melodramatic, but it's a melodramatic situation . . . '

'There's only one flaw in that neat theory, angel.'

'What?'

'You forget that I was at the funeral. I saw Bert Price. He wasn't my brother.'

The neat theory crumbled in my

hands. We were left once more with a shadowy ghost.

'Your brother . . . I get, somehow, the impression of an intense dislike, a hatred of him, pervading the valley, even the house — although his name was never brought to the surface very much. Did you dislike him, Thalia?'

'I must be honest, I suppose. I loved, and then hated him. But I wouldn't want him to be a murderer.'

She paused again.

'There's something else I think I should tell you,' she said. 'It's about David, the servant who was murdered.'

'Yes?'

'Desmond was his brother. Samantha was his wife. I have been living in a world surrounded by the past.'

The rain had stopped a little while before. Already it was much warmer. The night was very still now.

I tried to get back to a matter-of-fact conversation.

'Let's just look at things sensibly, Thalia. You don't want your family name to be dragged through the mud again,

149

and I don't blame you. But have you any cause really for fear? Look at the facts. Your brother disappeared, and the indications very strongly are that he was drowned. He hasn't been seen again on this farm, so how could he have moved so easily about it? He couldn't know what was in Judith's mind. He couldn't know where she would be on that evening. I think he's best left, drowned.

'But let's look at some of the other possibilities. Someone in the valley knows this story, knows both about the gold and, possibly, about the books, and sets a story on foot about a ghost. Judith possibly had her own value — what she could learn through her husband. But she comes too close for any sort of comfort. She's removed. It didn't take much strength, only surprise, to do it. The stories of the ghost are skilfully stirred. Where? How? We don't know.'

'The killer clearly was someone not on this farm. They were all here, remember.'

'Only from about five o'clock onwards. And Judith, when she was found, could have been dead for several hours.'

The silence was throbbing out at us, and Waif began his soft whimpering. Tiger sat up, his ears pricking. Soon Elsie would have hysterics. Thalia set about quietening them, and made preparations for going to bed.

'Be careful, Thalia,' I said.

'You bet! I'm taking Tiger with me for protection — I can't face crossing even that bit of courtyard.'

Just before we parted a sound came down the valley, first a low rumble, then a mighty roar.

'Oh, my God,' said Thalia. 'That's the river again, coming down worse than before. Now any local motor boats or canoes will have been lost, and the net result is — we've been cut off properly, this time.'

Shortly after that we went to bed.

★ ★ ★

In the light of the gas I began looking at my dusty books. The contents of most of them were also as dry as dust. Despite my apprehension, I found myself drifting off. Tiredly, only half-thinking, I put my torch

151

on the bed beside me, and turned off the gas.

I was surrounded by the small sounds of the night, the chirruping of the crickets, the hoarse bass of the bull frogs in the furrow near the dam. Outside, the skies had cleared and the stars were gleaming with a glossy, luminous light, as though they, too, had been made wet by the inundation.

I then plunged head first into sleep.

I was awakened by a slight stirring of sound. One of the books on the table next to me had moved.

I lay quietly, scarcely breathing. Something else seemed to be pausing. My hand was next to my torch. I switched it on.

But I was not quick enough. I was only in time to see the white shadow of an arm withdraw itself quickly from my window, like a snake sucked back into its hole. I was at the window in a flash but whoever it was had disappeared behind the wall.

Then I was outside, having forgotten the danger. But I could see and hear nothing. Only the throbbing silence.

Not one of the dogs had barked.

8

I must have slept, because I awoke to another dazzlingly bright day. The sun had flipped its dark side, and lay beaming light and heat onto us.

But the waters had risen. I could now see them from the window of my rondawel. We were well and truly on an island; worse, indeed, than other islands because the people here were not accustomed to boats, and few possessed even a plank to float on.

Though I had been shaken by the shadowy episode of the previous night, and though all that had happened had stirred me into a condition of restless apprehension, I could still enjoy the green, golden heat. The lawns and bushes shone like velvet, studded with diamonds and pearls. The birds were on the wing once again. A dove perched in a tree near me, giving its sound to the morning.

'Coo-ce-roo-coo-coo!'

The brilliant kingfisher returned to the window frame, his sharp eyes fixed on the activities of a cluster of fairy insects. I moved almost luxuriously in my bed, almost with well-being.

The uneasiness had passed, and its place had been taken by a more substantial feeling. Certain facts had solidified. The vague fear had become an actual one: the beast was still on the farm, and it could move in such a way that not even dogs were disturbed. Something seemed even clearer. The shadow had already learned of the distribution of Judith's books, and it seemed that I had in my part of the collection something it wanted badly. If I had left my door unlocked, it might even have ventured into the room itself.

But why wait till so late at night — unless that was the only time it had in which to reach the farm? I had left my room unguarded for a long time while I was talking to Thalia. Then I remembered: the door had been locked, and the windows had been secured against the storm. It was only when I went to bed late that night that I had opened the window. It couldn't of course get in because of the bars.

I smiled grimly to myself. That at least disposed of the ghost theory.

This thing wanted something on my table very much, so much so that it risked stretching its arm through the window towards me. A white arm? A black arm? Though I had the sensation of a white shadow, the sudden light as it caught it could have given this effect to black or white. The snake had simply been too quick for me.

★　★　★

Breakfast was being served on the stoep when I emerged. The sun fell across the golden swazi mat, the shadows of the poinsettias with their crimson candelabra flowers fell in blue designs on the grey cement floor. Sunlight washed into the bowls of the paw-paws that had been cut, and across the scrubbed white-wood table. Outside was the green veld, and beyond that the water. Bloedplaas was

155

even more poignantly beautiful than before.

Eric and Mrs. Hardwood were both drawing, she was at her trees, he doing rapid studies of faces. How quickly these artists could recover their spirits! As I passed I glanced at their drawings and received something of a shock. She was drawing a thick gathering of thorn-trees, made secret by the long grass between them, the thick clusters of blossom, the mesh of the big bush spiders. It was in a place such as this that Judith had been found.

Eric was doing studies of our faces. We were all there: the shadow of Tony's expression, the severe lines of Monica's set face. I stared at myself, not particularly pleased by what I saw. Charmaine had her mouth open; Samuel had his shut. Mrs. Hardwood's eyes were masked by the glint of her spectacles. Thalia, was in the foreground, with the dark faces of her servants, Desmond and Samantha, behind her. There were the Braaks too — the rough texture of their skins barely suggested: her bold, unfrightened eyes;

his, by contrast, were small and shifty. A veritable rogues gallery, I told myself.

The paw-paw was good, the fried egg and bacon delicious. I knew that already I had begun to forget Judith. But Monica hadn't. I could see it in the glazed way in which she walked as she came down with Thalia, Elsie and Tiger padding beside them. She ate almost nothing, staring moodily into her plate. The two artists took little notice of her. She ignored Tony. The party was becoming a complex and difficult one.

We had almost finished when Charmaine appeared, accompanied by Mrs. Braak. The young woman seemed flustered and fearful, the older completely composed.

'I suppose I had to come back!' she broke out. 'Can't we get out of this place, Samuel?'

'I've been trying to explain to the child that we won't be out of this for days, and she'll have to make the best of it,' Mrs. Braak interpolated matter-of-factly. Something, however, was gleaming in her eyes. She looked at us curiously, one face after the other.

'Make the best of murder! Aren't the roads better than you think?'

'I'm afraid it's much worse than we thought,' said Thalia. 'Not only are the roads lost to us, but also the canoe. I sent Desmond to the jetty this morning. He couldn't get near it, only near enough to see that the jetty's covered in water, that there's no sign of a boat, and that the current's flowing strongly.'

'Oh God!' said Charmaine. 'Have we got to sit here to be picked off one by one?'

After breakfast I got Sergeant Combrink and Thalia alone. I told them what had happened that night.

'I wonder,' he mused. 'Have those books got the answer?'

'What I can't understand is why the dogs weren't roused. Tiger's a good watchdog, Waif even a better one.'

'Part of that mystery can be explained,' said Thalia. 'The other part is dark to me, and I'm worried about it. Tiger wasn't stirred because he was in my rondawel with the two of us, and Elsie. The door was closed and he wouldn't have heard a sound if it was reasonably minute. I don't know why Waif wasn't stirred, but I do know that he's not here. He hasn't put in an appearance this morning. Desmond hasn't seen him either.'

'Where could he be?'

'He used to be a waif and stray, as you know. He's very timid. Something may have happened to scare him out of his wits.'

'But wouldn't he have whimpered, wailed?'

'I don't know what we're up against, that's the trouble: this seems to be more than an evil person — an influence, a shadow. I only hope Waif comes in later in the morning.'

Sergeant Combrink spoke, following his own line of thought.

'Did Dr. Thurle, to your knowledge, leave the rondawel?'

'Yes, she did. She got up to go to the lavatory. I offered to go with her, but she seemed contemptuous of, no that's not the word — indifferent to, my cowardice. She went on her own.'

'Did the dogs go with her?'

'I kept them back in the rondawel. She said I should.'

'What time was this?'

'I don't quite know. My watch had stopped. It certainly wasn't 9.30. That's what it said.'

'What time did your visitor come, Mr. Digby?'

'I'm afraid I couldn't tell you, sergeant. I just didn't think of looking at my watch.'

He made us feel highly inadequate witnesses.

I went back to the stoep. I was perturbed about Waif. He certainly couldn't have got far, with the water spread out as it was. I began to walk about the farm-house, calling ... My voice seemed like the plaintive beating of the wooddove.

Waif was nowhere to be found.

Eric and Mrs. Hardwood spent the morning drawing. Monica stared emptily across the water. She had forgotten about her medical tomes. She appeared to me to have been deprived of motive and life, and moved like an automaton. I was almost touched by her hardness, by a suffering so intense that it couldn't suffer properly.

Just before lunch I had reason to speak to Thalia and Combrink again. This meeting took place next to one of the magnolia trees a little to the side of the house. Combrink seemed to have become more and more fearful of being over-heard. Apprehension and caution in that rough man were disconcerting.

Our conversation was laced by the intense, sweet smell of the magnolia tree. It was full at that time of year, with waxen, ivory blossoms, almost, it seemed to me, sweeter, more poignant, than life itself.

'I must confess to you people,' Combrink scratched his chin, 'that I'm stymied by this case. I don't know how to go on. I need help from experts. Obviously I can't get it. Perhaps I should arrest you all.' There was the beginning of a grim smile. 'But what am I to do with you then? No, there's no way out of it. I need — as the detectives would say — a clue. I know your story, Miss du Mont. It doesn't take me any further. Someone comes in the night. We don't hear that person, a person who casually tries to remove a few books for light reading.

'I've found out the background of those people there.' He indicated the five sitting on the stoep. 'There are perhaps a few shadows — long ones in Mrs. Hardwood's case — but they don't add up to a crime. Dr. Thurle obsessed with her medicine, and with Mrs. Price. Doesn't seem to like men much, and blames young Tony Reade for Mrs. Price's death. She called you a murderer that first night, but she told me she didn't mean it. She seems to have developed an intense jealousy, amounting to hatred, for young Reade. Mrs. Price took notice of him, I understand.

'Mr. Shackleton was fairly indifferent, by his own confession, to Mrs. Price. Couldn't quite understand what young Reade saw in her — he liked Mrs. Hardwood much more. Young Reade, on the other hand, seems to have developed quite a passion for the dead woman; I would . . . '

This was his characteristic hesitation

before an announcement.

'I would be inclined to call it love. Take the Smiths now — there's a queer, ordinary couple for you. She's almost too stupid to be true, except, I think, her resentments — for this place, for you Miss du Mont, for Dr. Thurle. They are shallow, but quite violent nevertheless. Her husband is a convenience to her; she doesn't mind how uncomfortable she makes him, as long as she doesn't have to worry about anything. He's almost too ordinary the other way again — nothing to say for himself, although I'm sure he does his job well. His position as an accountant seems a good one. He indulges his wife in order to achieve peace for himself. He thinks his own thoughts, but doesn't worry too much about thinking outside his calling.

'Now what about old Braak and his wife. He knows the valley, he can easily circulate rumours about a ghost, he was interested in the gold diggings at one time. He's enormously wealthy. The question is, would he kill for money? Unless he wanted more, of course. Your servants, Desmond particularly? I would say this was not a Bantu crime, but Desmond learnt skill working for your father and he's not a fool, Miss du Mont. Samantha has a reason for revenge — but what sort of a revenge could this have been? That possibility doesn't make sense.

'And then there's the Braak servant, the unknown Rinka. I'll have to have a look at her soon. But there you are, no leads. I'm stuck in the mud.'

'Let's have lunch,' said Thalia, proposing one of her more common solutions. 'Perhaps we should continue with the search through our books. And I keep on worrying about poor Waif.'

'He hasn't come, then?' said the sergeant, the light in his eyes seeming to flicker. 'He didn't make a sound last night when our visitor came. That's queer, you know.'

He scratched his chin again.

Once more we were a silent party at lunch, Thalia and Eric doing most of the talking.

I had made up my mind that after the

meal I would continue perusing my books. A chance discovery sent me off in another direction altogether.

After leaving the luncheon table I had gone for a short stroll across the lawn. As I looked out beyond the avenue, beyond the haunt of the wood owls, I saw something strange, a large shape like a crocodile, on the edge of the water. I didn't say anything to anyone, but went down to see what it was. I realised then that I wouldn't get very far in the mud, and went back to change into shorts. By then the company on the stoep had dispersed, each to their own rondawel, or wherever they were going. Many of them wouldn't venture very far from the house, I was sure of that.

I set off again for the avenue. Soon I was squelching through mud up to my knees. The clouds were beginning to come over again, though they didn't look as angry as they had on those two previous occasions. When I got to the edge of the water, the sky was already a heavy leaden colour, and the water where it wasn't muddy-brown had a soft leaden gleam, like dirty silver.

It wasn't a log of wood, after all, and it wasn't a crocodile. It was Desmond's canoe that the flood waters had taken off and, by a strange quirk, had deposited virtually on our doorstep. The oars had been tied on and they were both intact. I emptied out the water, and began pushing the canoe across the liquid mud to where the stream seemed to be flowing strongly. I hadn't a definite idea in my mind, but already the notion had gathered that I would set off rowing across the water, not to the bridge and the outside world, but to the vlei. Why there, I don't quite know — but I thought, vaguely, that there I would get a better view of the farm and, somehow, get things into perspective.

I was wet with perspiration by the time I had got the boat to anything that could really be called water. I gave it a push, jumped in and went sailing like a swan into the floods.

Soon I was well beyond the farm-house, paddling into the deeper water. Curiously, the stronger currents seemed to have faded, and I started cruising in and out of the yellow clumps of grass, watching the birds about me.

The egrets had settled in ghostly white colonies on branches groping out of the water. There were other birds too: finches, weaving in and out of the yellow clumps of grass; then the wild ducks, with their bobbing heads, as though they were on a family picnic. I saw, too, a few field mice, clinging to the mud wedged between the yellow clumps.

The sky had grown even more leaden. The grass and the water about me gleamed in suggestive pastel colours. The swifts had come out with the early evening, and were winging above in wild, mad loops against the sky, their split tails signals of animal triumph. Peering across the water I saw Thalia's home crouched in the Jacaranda and Kaffirboom trees. A sole hawk was gliding through the upper currents.

Then, weaving in and out of the clumps as I was, I thought the corner of my eye caught a movement not related to bird life. An arm had moved an oar in a partly obscured boat ahead of me. I paddled on as quickly as I could, lost what it was for a moment, and then way ahead I saw the canoe pause, a dim back bent, something was dropped into the water, again the movement of an arm. The canoe and its hazy occupant disappeared. I tried for several minutes to follow, but I could see and hear nothing, only the paddling of my own boat and the washing of the water amongst the reeds and grass.

I hesitated in midstream. Should I pursue my elusive copaddler, or try to find what it was that he had deposited? I didn't fancy a struggle amidst the reeds, if this was someone sinister — but that wasn't really the reason I didn't continue the pursuit. A need to see what it was that had been dumped possessed me.

I paddled back trying to decide at what reed clump the canoer had paused. But I was totally lost, going round and round on my tracks, creating whirlpools of sultry light, seeming to pass the same clump repeatedly. Not only had I lost my strange companion, not only had I mislaid his burden, but if I went on in this manner I myself would be in danger of being lost in the watery maze, for the sky was growing steadily more sullen.

I stopped uncertainly, not knowing what to do now. Then a brief, vigorous eddy in the water brought a small object to the surface and lodged it near a reed bank ahead. I paddled towards it, but it was lost to me again. But I knew where I had seen it sink and I reached down, my hands groping in the water and mud. I touched something solid, covered with hair. It escaped me, sank away. I reached again, found it, pulled it to the surface, and started in horror at what I had found. Poor Waif's stiff black hair was shiny with water, his puzzled eyes staring.

His throat had been very neatly cut.

9

After the first shock of having the small black body in my hands, I was consumed with rage. The cruelty, the wanton destruction of so inoffensive a creature filled me with loathing. Anything that stood in the path of a monstrous greed had to be destroyed. Waif's little head lolled over to one side as my hands shook.

I now paddled furiously, setting out towards the firm ground beyond the vlei. This thing must be caught before further evil could be set afoot. But my progress was slow and I was hampered by the many turnings amidst the reeds. The sky was even more leaden; sometimes visibility was sharp, then again you wondered whether you were not imagining things in that white-grey light, seeing a figure, a canoe, which turned out to be a log or a reed clump.

Yet, as I drew towards the bank, there *was* a figure ahead, standing beside the water, looking out towards Thalia's home and beyond that to the Valley of the Braaks. I came on it, out of another sweep of gloom. The person turned towards me. I saw that it was a tall African woman, her face that of a prophetess.

'It is gone, gone!' she cried, her voice ringing across the water. That strange ripple ran down my back once again.

She saw the body of Waif in the canoe.

'The ghost has made its passage,' she wailed. 'It has left the trail of the beast as it moves to the house.'

I recognised her then. I had seen this woman before, at the Braak's home. This was the unknown extra in the case, the mysterious Rinka.

As I moored the canoe and climbed out with Waif's body, she wailed once more:

'We are alone with the ghost, shut off by the waters.'

'What are you doing here, Rinka?' I asked sharply.

She looked sideways at me, an expression of grotesque cunning on her face.

'I have been following the ghost,' she said.

'Why?'

'Because, master, I have the powers of my people. I am wise: I have the medicine to trap the ghost.'

One of Mrs. Braak's anecdotes about her servants came back to me. This Rinka had the reputation of a mighty witch-doctor, one of the most renowned, it seemed, in the valley. She had the eccentricities of her calling, but she suited Mrs. Braak, who though she never tired of complaining about her servants, insisted on having Rinka near her at all times. The black woman was a source of information about what was going on in the surrounding valleys, both amongst white and black people. Mrs. Braak thrived on local lore and gossip. It was she who had first recounted the story of the appearance of the ghost.

I changed my line of attack. Pursuit, I saw, was hopeless because the gloom was swirling in quickly; already in the distance I could see the twinkle of Thalia's lights.

'You saw the ghost then?'

'Yes, I have seen the ghost.'

'Who was it?'

'Who can tell who ghosts are, until they are under the spell?'

'Was it a woman or a man?'

'I do not know, master. Ghosts are not men or women. I saw only the shadow of this ghost as it passed on its way to the water.'

She had not really seen our visitor, of that I was convinced, although she retained her look of cunning.

'Did you follow it down to the water, there?' I said, pointing to where I had found my canoe.

She gave me my first real piece of information.

'No, there.' She pointed in almost the opposite direction, past what had been the jetty, to what can be described as the head of the vlei. Our mysterious visitor had found the boat there. He — I had given the ghost a sex because I kept linking him with Thalia's brother — must have known where to look. That, too, was clear.

'You'd better start off home,' I said.

We trudged along together, an incongruous pair.

When we parted at Thalia's home Rinka raised her hand like a prophetess.

'Beware of the snake in the night!' she cried, and disappeared into the gloom. Her melodramatic gesture was completely in keeping. Nothing that had happened, or was to happen, seemed ridiculous any longer.

I found Sergeant Combrink inside with the others, and took him out onto the lawn where I had put Waif. He flashed his torch, bending over the body.

'It's the same person all right,' he said. 'The same neat job.'

He looked up at me.

'And this explains why no dogs barked in the night. Miss du Mont had the two with her. This one was neatly taken care of before he could give any warning.'

'Do you mean to say he got up to him and killed him, without the dog barking or whining?'

'He must have the step of a panther,' said Combrink. 'Or, otherwise, the dog knew him, well.'

I had not missed the growing definition of sex.

'You, too, think it's a man.'

'Oh, yes. All the indications I can see are that way. Yet . . . '

He paused, before speaking again.

'I wouldn't say there wasn't the touch of a woman in this. The audacity, the swift movement seem a man's, but the throat cutting, almost delicate, almost — feminine.'

Then he shrugged.

'Of course that's just how it seems to a slow chap, someone who hasn't got very far with this case. I just hope — nothing else is going to happen.'

'Do you think it will?'

'Look, man: we're looking for someone; that someone knows we're looking for him. Meanwhile, frantically now, I guess, he's looking for something else again, and he has to keep it dark from us. Or perhaps there's no search on his side; someone's simply trying to get something out of his system.'

'What do you mean?'

'What I mean is that it becomes continually more possible that we have a maniac on our hands. Either that or a person obsessed with his search for something, or . . . '

His pause was a speculative one.

'Or it may be a combination of both. That — ' he paused again, 'may be the most dangerous of all: cunning, madness, need, revenge, How many of these things are working in *that* mind?'

The night had become very dark.

I felt even less at ease when we went into the brightly lit sitting-room. Any of these people — Mrs. Hardwood, masked behind her spectacles; Eric, his head thrown back, a whisky at his mouth; Samuel attending his frightened, sulking wife; Tony, looking down, his face still in shadow; Monica, glassy as before. Even Thalia, with Desmond standing darkly behind her, waiting to announce that dinner had been served.

I went to bed early after dinner, because to search through the books had now become my main endeavour. I unlocked the rondawel, unbolted all the windows. The books were secure, untouched. I prayed that this would not be a night for mysterious visitors. There was so much to do.

I had spent over an hour on two extremely detailed and dull histories of the early Transvaal goldfields when I found what might have been my first clue, though it seemed minute. On the fly-leaf of the third book there was a faint, pencilled entry: 'p.57'. I turned immediately to that page. It was the beginning of a chapter, with a plate opposite. The plate was from an early photograph, taken, I guessed, some sixty years before. It was crude and the photograph faint. The picture was quite clearly a group of early miners, bearded, roughly clothed, standing in two rows. Underneath the photograph their names were printed. The opposite page was, as I said, the beginning of a chapter. It described the processes of gold panning, methods of washing out the alluvial findings of Eastern Transvaal streams. It was dull; there was nothing that I could find here even of remote interest.

I banged down the book in disgust, hardly having looked at it, and picked up the fourth book. I had a find almost immediately.

It fell open at a page, and I saw; with a quickening of pulse, why. A thin yellowed scrap of paper lay in between the pages. It consisted of some rough notes and a slight sketch; it had been made at least twenty years before. My latent romanticism stirred: it was like finding a treasure chart.

Strangely enough, it was just that. 'Here is my summary,' the note read. 'I have been through paper after paper, plan after plan, talked to people, picked up hints in the pubs. It does exist, of that I am sure now. It did not cross the border. It has not been lost. Several official despatches have given me the hint . . . '

There followed brief abstracts of these.

'One informal note,' it continued, 'missed by so many eyes has given me a definite pointer to its whereabouts. This is where it is.'

And here again were brief notes describing a small area near Pilgrim's Rest. On the back was a fairly clear map of its location. These seemed to me the jottings a man had kept to remind himself how to proceed once he had begun his quest.

I put the note under the books, closed the windows this time, switched off the gas lamp, and tried to get to sleep. But my mind was in turmoil, filled not with death and murder, but with whispers of treasure, the legends of the President's millions. Of course I should, strictly speaking, hand over the note, but I was reluctant to do so. Not that I wanted a treasure for myself, not that at all. But I had come to the conclusion that to tell anything to anyone was to put our mysterious, ruthless visitor on his guard and one step ahead of us. I wanted to test this particular idea for myself. But how? I was virtually on an island.

As I lay thinking, I hit on it. I had the canoe. Combrink in the bewilderment of the facts I had given him, seemed not to have tumbled to the fact that we were no longer marooned. We had a canoe at our disposal. Before anyone was up, before he realised this, I would use that canoe for myself, row across the flood water, go to old Mr. van der Stoop two miles above the bridge and borrow his jeep. I would need a jeep because the track shown on the map seemed to be an old, rough one. The tarred roads to Pilgrim's Rest should be quite safely above the flood waters.

I recalled something else. *He* too had a canoe, *he* too was not a prisoner on the farm. I must find it, destroy it, keep him prisoner, prevent him from following me. I didn't realise that by keeping a beast in captivity I could be making it wilder.

I tried once more to get to sleep.

I was up early before the farm had begun to stir. Tiger was on the stoep this time, but he was not alarmed by my sudden appearance. I had known him for several years in the course of my visits. He came up wagging his tail. I shut him inside the house, and made off as quickly as I could. I must have seemed a highly suspicious figure disappearing into the grey morning.

I had got to the boat when the sun began to rise. The dawn across the water was once again incongruously splendid, the fierce golden disc pushing itself up over the timber hills, pressing a golden suffusion into the sky, sending gigantic lighthouse beams rippling across the valley. I was a small shadow in a golden Turnerian painting.

I had pushed out into the reeds, which themselves were golden with sunlight. The sweet voice of the thrush came to me, and I saw the yellow stirring of the weavers. As I moved off I heard the throbbing noise of the doves. I was trying to follow the direction of Rinka's quivering finger — to reach the source of the creature's movement across the water, and destroy the canoe before I did anything else. The vlei narrowed at this point and led the waters up to a steep bank. Then I saw the end of the boat sticking out of the low-hanging bush that covered it. The place had been cunningly chosen, for here the flood waters were unlikely to reach unless they were very wild. The boat itself had been cleverly covered. I drew up next to it, searched it rapidly, found nothing, and then reached for the hammer and steel peg I had brought with me from my car.

If I had only thought for a moment I might have realised that here were valuable finger prints if other means of identifying our visitor failed. Alas, I didn't think that far. I only thought of destroying part of his terrible mobility. As it happened there were no means of testing finger prints on the farm, and this would eventually only have served as confirmation of what we came to know.

I spiked the peg on the floor of the canoe, then drove it in with the hammer. Pulled out the peg, hammered it in several times.

With a low, sucking noise the boat began to sink. As I moved away it was veering gently into the water, disappearing slowly. That means of transport would not be used again. I was now filled with a sense of urgency, and rowed rapidly towards the bridge. I had a clear sense of direction, if not of sight, because the bridge lay in the route of the dawn.

Twenty minutes passed. Eventually I drew in, and moored the boat where Desmond and I had done before. Then I was on the road, climbing up the hill to Mr. van der Stoop's homestead. The old man was surprised to see me, for the story of the valley had reached him. He knew my books, however, and trusted me. He didn't question me much. Soon I was shooting off towards Pilgrim's Rest in his jeep. The sunlight was mixing with the vapours of the valley: the jeep seemed to be forging its way through a fine golden mesh. I remembered the previous occasion on which we had undertaken this journey, all of us in two cars. Had the Sinister One been among us then?

I had certainly felt it, but perhaps it was simply the spirit of the Braak Valley travelling with us.

Graskop fell away on one side of the speeding vehicle. Within about two hours of leaving Mr. van der Stoop I got to the outskirts of Pilgrim's Rest. I would have to drive carefully now if I was not to miss my turning. I stopped the jeep and scrutinised the map. By my reckoning the turning-off should be about two miles ahead, leading left into the hills. I started off again, climbing along the road towards the crest that bordered the town.

I was right. There it was, a mere track entering darkly into the bush. Thank God I had a jeep. A car would never have succeeded in those ruts, up the sharp, fierce inclines, and with the multitude of loose stones about. This was a nightmare though minor journey, the jeep bouncing under me, the steering wheel struggling to take its own course. I kept it to the road with all the tenacity I could muster, pushing it on and upwards. The four miles I travelled seemed longer than the rest of the journey put together, but at last I could see that the bush was thinning out. I got to a space where there were quite clearly signs of disused diggings. The small stream was below me over a rise; it had flattened out into a bowl of land, high above the town.

The indications of the map were all being fulfilled. I moved to a small head of ground overlooking the kloof. The flat stone, with one sharp gash on top was there. Though the note had said 'not too deep down', I had taken the precaution of bringing a spade with me. I lifted the stone and began digging. A foot down. I had to rest because I was trembling with exhaustion — and excitement. I had written about the President's millions several times, but could never bring myself to believe in their existence. The legend was coming true. This was a real adventure story which had left a trail of blood and madness in its wake.

I started digging again. As I did so I felt the presence of Rinka and her maledictions, the presence of all the old ghosts of the diggings, of those who had pursued the millions, Thalia's father and brother, perhaps Mr. Braak, Bert Price. More than any of these people I felt the presence of the ghost, the vague shadowy figure with a scalpel in its hand. It was then almost tangible.

I went on digging even more fiercely, and struck something in the true tradition of treasure-trove stories. I quickly uncovered the top of the small tin box — it was not more than a foot wide and two feet long. I hauled it up.

There was no lock to it, and as I snapped it open I could see that there was nothing inside. Except a piece of paper which I took out, sick with disappointment.

A laconic message had been printed in large letters on the paper:

'Too late'.

10

'You've got a lot to answer for,' said Combrink. His look was steely.

I had come in about mid-morning, stowed my boat under some long grass, and then gone direct to where he and Thalia sat together in the sitting-room. Thalia's look could hardly have been described as friendly. I must say I couldn't blame either of them. All the way back I was possessed by the enormous stupidity of what I had done. I had thought I would find a quick, clever solution, but I had been thwarted by someone much more clever.

Eric and Mrs. Hardwood were under a tree, drawing. Both Tony and Monica were watching them. Samuel was to one side on the stoep, reading. I was later to understand that Charmaine had gone back to Mrs. Braak, that she was showing her a large scrap album she had brought with her of snapshots, old letters, cuttings. I had seen part of this album and had found it interminably boring, especially the explanations by Charmaine that accompanied each of the entries. Mrs. Braak, apparently, was fascinated by her guest. She certainly fitted into the ball and claw and wall to wall circle. That shows you what a feeble snob I am!

I turned from the window to my two accusers.

'I know I've done an unforgivable thing,' I said. 'I may even be under suspicion myself.'

'You're telling me,' said Combrink curtly.

'Let me explain everything that's happened. Believe me, I seek few excuses for myself. I deserve your censure. But I thought that by going off like this I'd get fewer people involved.'

I then told them my story. They listened attentively enough. When I had finished Combrink said, this time not as unkindly as before:

'Well, let's see your bits of paper.'

I produced the directions and plan that had taken me to Pilgrim's Rest, and also the note in block letters that announced that I was too late.

'This note,' said Thalia, picking up the directions, 'is in my father's handwriting. I'm absolutely certain of that. The other, of course, I'd have a great deal of difficulty in identifying. But I've seen that sort of lettering before — let me think about it for a moment.'

'Could it be our visitor's?' I asked.

'I'm almost sure that it isn't — I haven't seen it recently.'

'The paper,' said Combrink fingering it, 'is far from new.'

'Could it be your brother's?'

'Again I'm almost sure it isn't. But let me get one of his letters.'

She went off and brought back one of André's last letters to her. The handwriting was markedly different from that of her father's.

'That's not it, I'm sure,' she said.

'While we're on the subject of letters, let's put out Mrs. Price's as well.'

He drew it from his pocket and spread it out on the table.

'Not that it will help.'

But as I saw Judith's handwriting again something did stir in me. I had seen that type of script somewhere.

'I've got it!' Thalia said suddenly.

We looked up at her.

'That block lettering. Of course, I've seen it on packages so many times. But it was long ago.'

'Well?' said Combrink.

'There's no doubt about it: it's my father's lettering.'

For some reason we felt deflated. This was the past again, not the present, not even the past reaching into the present in the form of the mysterious André, or the shadowy Bert Price.

'That means of course,' said Combrink slowly, 'that your father found whatever was in that chest, and removed it.'

'It would be like him,' said Thalia, 'to put the box back in the hole, and to leave a monstrously whimsical note such as that. He had a wry sense of humour.'

'It also means,' said Combrink, 'that someone may have known this, and was trying to prise his secret from him.'

He turned to Judith's letter again.

'If you remember, Mrs. Price said that she had found and kept some notes. These perhaps took the search to the end of the trail.'

'Why perhaps?' I asked, having got his emphasis.

'Because our visitor, as far as I can see, shows no signs of giving up. He's still looking, isn't he?'

'We don't know. All that we know is that he has to stay here because he can't leave.'

'But he could leave, you know, until you took a hand in the matter. I'm afraid the boat you so neatly sank may have given us the clue to his identity. Not only finger prints, but he may finally have tried, if the temptation was there, to run for it.'

He looked at me accusingly. I felt appropriately miserable.

'But I don't think he would have tried that,' he qualified, 'because of my hunch. Besides, the water and mud wouldn't have left many finger prints.'

I didn't, of course, deserve kindness.

'What is it Mrs. Price says again?' He

picked up the letter. '' . . . I came across a document . . . A location was given.' Now would that be the old spot, or the new one?'

As he put the letter down, I saw Judith's handwriting once again. Once again I had a flickering of recognition.

I was about to say something when the rear door of the sitting-room crashed open. Mrs. Braak and Charmaine, the scrap-book under an arm, burst in.

'I couldn't let the child come on her own,' Mrs. Braak explained. She looked out of the window. 'Ach, there your husband is, child. He must be worried about you. Go to him.'

'Thank you for a lovely day, Mrs. Braak,' said Charmaine demurely. She drifted towards the stoep.

I glanced out of the window myself. Her husband didn't seem particularly animated by her re-appearance, but she talked away at him and seemed not to notice his reaction.

'How are you people getting on with this murder?' Mrs. Braak confronted us. 'That's what I wanted to see you about, sergeant. How long are you going to let us people in this valley live with a murderer? It's not right, you know.'

'I'm doing my best, madam,' the sergeant replied evenly.

She was evidently not completely restored to good humour by Charmaine's visit.

'But your best's not good enough!' she burst out.

Just as suddenly, her aggression vanished. She had come close to the table and was looking down at the various papers. There was an abstracted expression on her face. It was almost instantly replaced by a screen of cunning.

'Who wrote this?' she asked, stabbing out at the directions and plan.

'My father.'

'And this?' Stabbing at André's letter.

'My brother.'

Thalia clearly wanted to be rid of the woman as soon as possible.

'And this?' This time at Judith's.

'Stop,' said Combrink. 'You've no right to ask these questions, Mrs. Braak. You mustn't answer them, Miss du Mont.'

'Let her know,' said Thalia carelessly. 'Judith Price wrote the letter.'

Thalia's indifference, more than the sergeant's abruptness, put a match to the tinder of the older woman's resentment. Mrs. Braak burst into flame, verbal that is, her face a fiery red.

'You and your superior airs, Talie du Mont! You make me sick! Do you think I don't know about you and your family — that fine brother of yours. A murderer! even if it was only a farm kaffir he killed. He was a liar, a cheat! Those millions. My husband had been looking, too. And the agreement was that whoever first found them it was share and share alike. But I tell you this . . . '

Her voice was raised, and I could see those on the stoep looking up at the window.

'There's going to be more blood let loose in this valley by the time I've had my say!'

'I think you'd better keep quiet,' said Combrink.

'Who are you to tell me what to do? You're such a good cop, aren't you? You

194

can't even see what's clear to me.'

'You'd better leave, madam.'

'Yes, I will leave, but you haven't seen the last of me, nor you Miss Talie du Mont! There are still going to be some very interesting discussions, I can tell you that.'

Like a fury she disappeared through the back door. The fiery serpent was sucked into the hole of the night. We were left sitting somewhat stunned in her wake.

'What could have brought that on?' said Thalia quietly, but quite evidently crushed. 'I knew she disliked my family, disliked me — but I honestly thought we were getting beyond that.'

'Where there's so much greed and jealousy, there's got to be hatred,' said Sergeant Combrink. 'She suddenly tumbled to the bigness of what she and her husband had been cheated of.'

He paused.

'Well, we'd better put these away before there's more harm done.'

'Just a moment,' I said. 'Let me see that letter of Judith's again.'

I inspected the handwriting carefully.

'I now have my moment of recognition,' I said. 'It's only a pencilled entry, 'p.57' I think, in one of the books you gave me to go through. But I'll bet my bottom dollar that that entry was in Judith's handwriting. Let me get the book.'

'No,' said Sergeant Combrink quietly. 'We've already made enough mistakes by our indiscretion. I'll have to look at that book in your room tonight, Mr. Digby. Not now, please.'

He turned to Thalia.

'If you feel a little better, Miss du Mont, I think we'd better have that supper the boy promised. Afterwards we should make sure, Mr. Digby, that that boat of yours is safe.'

★   ★   ★

After supper Combrink and I walked beneath the silver moonlight to the vlei. Again it lay like a burnished silver shield in front of us.

'The Braak woman obviously knows

something,' he said as we trudged along. 'She's greedy, and she seems to have begun smelling gold again. Money's power to her. She's going to raise the valley to get it.'

'Where will it end?'

'Though I must admit that I haven't been very clever in this case, I have an idea that this thing . . . '

As usual the pause.

' . . . this curse is working itself out. As long as no one puts a foot wrong now. And that's what I'm afraid the Braak woman's going to do. At all costs we must prevent further bloodshed.'

With those words the finger had returned to my back. I shivered in a night recovering from the violence of the storm.

'And that's why,' he continued, 'I want to make sure about this boat of yours. We must have an escape route. There must be a contact with the outside world, because I just don't know what the outside world's doing about us. I don't want to leave the farm at present, but tomorrow I may have to go in and shake things up a bit. We should be near your boat now, shouldn't we?'

Our boots were already sinking deep into mud.

'Yes.'

And just as I said it I heard a sound, a sliding and then a soft plash.

I started running clumsily, kicking up heavy bootfuls of mud and water.

'Quick!' I cried. 'I think someone's at the boat.'

We were both clawing clumsily ahead to the edge of the water.

Once again we were too late. The boat had set out, only twenty yards or so in front of us. It was being paddled deftly through the reed banks.

'Stop, do you hear!' Combrink shouted ineffectually into the night.

We were answered by a soft throaty chuckle before the boat disappeared behind a clump of reeds. It was not seen again. The mysterious boatsman had disappeared.

★ ★ ★

We trudged back disconsolately, dismayed by yet another failure. A near miss, but a failure.

'Well, at least we'll be able to see who's on the farm now,' said Combrink. 'In a way I hope the bird — the vulture shall we call him — has flown. That'll indentify him, and, perhaps . . . leave us safe.'

Eric and Mrs. Hardwood were in the sitting-room when we returned. They were once more at their drawings. We found Thalia with Desmond in the kitchen, doing the last clearing up for the evening. At our request he went off to the servant's quarters, returning with Samantha.

We began a tour of the rondawels. Samuel was in bed. Charmaine was sitting beside him, showing him the scrap-book she had brought back with her from Mrs. Braak. Tony was in his room, trying to write a letter. Quite clearly, he was not succeeding. The last rondawel was Monica's.

There was no answer as we knocked. We knocked again.

I felt cold fear, but more than this, a

sickness with life.

'Not her,' I kept saying to myself. 'Not her.'

Sergeant Combrink tried the door, and it opened. Monica *was* there, staring into the hurricane lamp, not seeming to have heard us. Then she looked up and saw me. She said something strange.

'Thank God.'

The shutters dropped again, and she addressed us both blankly.

'What do you want?'

'Nothing,' said Combrink. 'Goodnight.'

'We must get to the Braaks,' he said. Once more we were stumbling through the haziness, the bright moon helping us on our way. We trudged through the ornamental garden, crazy in the moon-light with its dwarfs and dragons, across the pseudo-gracious patio of The Grape-vine, up to the ornamental door. Sergeant Combrink knocked loudly, without ceremony.

There was a distinct lapse of time before it opened. Mrs. Braak stood before us stony-eyed, in a long unelegant dressing gown, her hair in two thick plaits.

'What do you want?' she seemed to be repeating Monica's question.

The sergeant could be equally abrupt.

'Where's your husband?'

'He's in bed.'

'May I see him, please.'

'He's asleep.'

'Your servant?'

'I've just seen that she's safely locked herself in her bedroom. I'm not calling her either. We're scared enough without anything else happening to rouse us, particularly the girl.'

'Can you give me your word that they're here?'

'Of course.'

'All right. Keep them safe, please.'

As we walked back, he commented.

'That makes it look as if this 'thing' has not been in either of the two households. It's been skulking around, hiding in the valley like the ghost they've described. It could be the brother after all — that story becomes more and more likely. He would know of places even to live, caves; he would know where to hide the boat.'

I was not completely enamoured of the brother theory.

'I don't want to teach you your job, sergeant,' I said, 'particularly after the mess I've made today. But don't you think you should have insisted on seeing Mr. Braak?'

'She couldn't get away with a lie like that, you know. We'd soon know whether Braak was on the farm or not. Then she'd really be in trouble. She knows that.'

'But she *was* lying. I've known Mrs. Braak on and off for a long time, and I'm sure she was lying. There was something in her manner that to me simply wasn't right.'

'And you're right,' he said. 'I should never let things go like this. What a bloody rotten sergeant I am. Come on! We're going back.'

Mrs. Braak had quite clearly been congratulating herself on our defeat. She was clearly shocked by our reappearance. The sergeant wanted to see her husband.

'All right,' she said. 'But don't wake him.'

He was in his bed, and seemed to be sleeping. We were both nonplussed.

'Where's the maid?'

'Look, this time take my word for it.'

'We want to see her.'

'All right. I hope she hears you. I've told her to cover her head with a blanket.'

The door was locked. We hammered loudly on it. There was no response.

'Look, she's fast asleep!'

'Get a key, please.'

'I'm not going to start looking for one now.'

The sergeant was determined this time.

'We'll have to break the door down.'

With that she went off to get a key, grumbling to herself. She handed it to him without saying anything. He slid it into the lock.

Rinka was not in her room.

★   ★   ★

'Where can she have gone?' said Mrs. Braak, suddenly dismayed, even apologetic. 'She must have sneaked out after I saw her to bed. Honestly, I didn't know she wasn't here.'

I was again almost certain she was lying. I said as much to Sergeant Combrink as we walked back to Thalia's farm.

'Yes, I reckon she was,' he said. 'But she was suddenly too scared by what she'd done for us to get anything but blank denials from her tonight. She'll have thought better of it in the morning — I hope.'

'Besides,' I added, 'she said she'd seen Rinka to bed only just before we came. But we saw the boat and its occupant — which was almost certainly Rinka — setting out fully an hour before.'

'Yes, it's a queer business.'

We had reached the house, and could see the orange lights of the rondawels blinking out at us, incongruously friendly.

'Let's have a look at that book of yours,' said Combrink.

In my rondawel we compared the two handwritings. There was no doubt that the pencilled 'p.57' was a note Judith had made. We turned to the page, carefully studied the faces in the plate, but recognised none of them — they were all very old, having been active well before the time even of Thalia's father. A period piece. We went through the page describing the panning of gold.

'It beats me,' Combrink said. 'I don't know why she marked this particular page. There's nothing much of interest here. Perhaps it was just an idle interest on her part. There are no other pages marked, you say?'

'No, there aren't.'

'Ah well, it couldn't have been important.'

He was right in a sense. It wasn't merely important. It was crucial. Our hands were on the truth and we couldn't find it.

'Well, I'll say goodnight,' he said, and added dryly: 'Pleasant dreams!'

I locked the door behind him. Quite soon afterwards I switched off the gas lamp. I was tired after my jaunt and went to sleep almost immediately. I did not expect the appearance of any visitors that night. I was wrong.

I was awakened by something landing

on my bed, crawling softly towards my face. I lay as if frozen, listening to the loud drumming of my blood. I reached out, touched the thing. I touched its fur.

That was too much for me. I sat up in bed and struck a match. I was almost overwhelmed by the anti-climax. It was Thalia's favourite cat, Libby.

'You slut!' I gasped with relief.

But how had she got there? I thought I had sealed myself in. I climbed out of bed and inspected the door and then the windows. One of the windows was swinging loosely on the wooden frame. It had, quite clearly, been prised open.

My collection of books was intact. I had remembered to take them off the table and put them under the bed.

11

The next morning was another golden day. Sergeant Combrink and I trudged up to The Grapevine once again. Mrs. Braak opened the door to us. She signalled us into her sitting-room.

'Where's your husband?'

'He's down looking at the damage to the lands. I wanted him to go.'

'Why?'

'I was expecting you,' she said leadenly.

It was clear that she hadn't slept. There were dark rings under her eyes, her anger had disappeared, her cunning seemed to have forsaken her.

The sergeant was brutally direct.

'You lied last night, didn't you.'

She was, it seemed, too tired to fight.

'Yes, I lied to you. It was I who sent Rinka out in the boat.'

'Okay, that's settled at least. Now we may be getting somewhere near the truth.'

She looked up quickly at him, the cunning blinking out of her eyes for a moment. Then she relapsed into lethargy.

'How did you know about the boat?'

'Rinka told me. There were, in fact, two she said. One she saw in the water, sunk. But yesterday afternoon she told me she had found the other.'

'Why did you send her?'

'I wanted help, from outside.'

'Your help hasn't come yet?'

She sighed heavily.

'It's quite clear to me that it won't come. Rinka wanted to get off this cursed farm, as she called it, back to her own people in the North. She won't come back, and now we have no boats . . . '

'What did you want help for?'

'For something I knew. I wanted justice.'

'What was it you knew?'

He was trying to be patient with her.

'Ah, that I won't tell, until there's justice done.'

He spoke urgently now.

'Do you realise, Mrs. Braak, that someone's been murdered because of your secret? That it could happen again?'

'I know.'

'And you're not going to talk? You may be in danger yourself.'

'I'm not frightened too much of the danger, but I am — very tired.'

She suddenly made up her mind.

'Look, let me try to get this straight to myself. Let me sort out my ideas. I'll come to see you at lunch-time. Not later than one o'clock, I promise you that.'

She was not to be budged, and we had to be satisfied. Back we went to Thalia's farm.

'It seems that our visitor is still with us,' the sergeant remarked.

★　★　★

The morning passed slowly. People wandered in and out. They seemed to have become slightly braver. Eric and Mrs. Hardwood went off beyond the dam to do their drawing. Tony decided to go to the river to bathe, and perhaps, I thought, to look at the place where he and Judith had been on that morning which now seemed so very distant. Could a day such as that ever return?

Charmaine was busy at her scrap-book once more, and insisted on drawing my attention to various tiresome items in it. There were notes written to her husband — she seemed to have asked for every single line back; there were snapshots and cuttings that he had patiently marked for her. He seemed embarrassed by the whole procedure, hastily donned a hat, and went walking off in the direction that Eric and Mrs. Hardwood had taken. Thalia and the two servants were working in the kitchen or in the large farmyard bordering on the servants' quarters. Monica kept, apparently, to her room. She was in bed, Thalia said, and seemed to be getting worse rather than better, moodier, more despondent. She didn't communicate easily, poor girl.

I was crossing to the dam when I was hailed back by an excited Charmaine.

'Oh, do come and look at this! I've come across some most interesting pages. I'm sure they'll interest you because of all this talk about gold and mining and treasures. And your books and all that. I wonder whether you've seen this material.'

I hadn't. It was a series of articles dealing with gold and its appearance in South Africa. In an article on the Eastern Transvaal, I came up short before a group photograph. It was much more recent than that that faced on the mysterious 'p.57', and I recognised several of the people. Two looked remarkably like Thalia, an older man and a younger. I glanced at the caption:

'Thomas du Mont. André du Mont.'

They stared at me from across time, the past in the present. Their secrets were the secrets of this wretched place. Their torments had become our torments.

Behind them, I recognised someone else. There was no doubt about it, and the caption confirmed this: Mr. Braak.

Yet another face seemed familiar. This, too, was confirmed by the caption: Albert Price.

Out of nine people four were very much part of our story. It was uncanny, disconcerting. Charmaine was looking at me gleefully. She could see that something she had produced had at last fascinated me. The smile remained on her face, but her eyes were closely watchful.

I tried to appear casual.

'Where in the world did you get hold of these? Why did you collect them?'

'I think Samuel must have given them to me. No, that's not true. I had them before I met Samuel. You see they're dated more than ten years ago.'

'But why did you make cuttings of them?'

'I was interested at the time.'

'Interested?'

'In gold. I was interested in the stories of lost gold. As a girl I had dreams of being rich. Also, someone had told me a lot about gold.'

She took a deep breath, then laughed a rather unpleasant laugh.

'How one gets caught out!'

She laughed again.

'You see, I knew Bert Price quite well. I see you've seen him in that photograph amongst the others. My questions to Judith about her husband, about how she was making out, were not, you see, as silly as you thought. I'm not quite the bird-brain you take me for. I remembered Bert, and I wanted to know more about what had happened to him?'

She tittered, again in not quite a pleasant way.

'I told Samuel about it afterwards. He was really surprised that I had known anything at all about what had gone on in this part of the world. I didn't of course know about the du Monts, or didn't remember, or I wouldn't have come here. This is a ghastly place.'

She shuddered violently. It seemed that a shadow had crossed the lawn. There were others then, for the scudding clouds were moving past the sun.

I had had enough of the woman.

'I think I'll go for my bathe,' I said, gathering up my towel and book. As I crossed the lawn I glanced back.

I could see that the unwise Charmaine was showing her scrap-book to Thalia.

I plunged in. The water was cold, mountain fresh. I came up gasping, turned the direction of my head quickly, felt I had been watched. I was probably becoming jumpy, over-sensitive. I forced myself to go on swimming, and I must say my muscles took fire from the water. I began to delight once more in the weavers building their nests, stripping the bamboo, and, sometimes, destroying the homes of others when they thought them undefended. I got out, and towelled myself off quickly. The party had been broken up for several hours now.

Both Thalia and Charmaine had disappeared. Looking below the embankment I could see that Eric, Samuel and Mrs. Hardwood had come together and were trudging back. I waited for them, and in a friendly manner they showed me their drawings. Mrs. Hardwood had gone further into the bush and she had one or two sketches of thorn-trees, rather more swiftly executed than usual, I thought. Eric's drawings were again lightning quick. One was of the lands below the Braak home; there, quite recognisable, was Mr. Braak toiling through his fields.

'You saw Mr. Braak, then?'

'Oh yes, I think he was walking up to

The Grapevine just then.'

'You haven't quite finished it. He's faceless.'

'Yes. I had stopped to take breath when Samuel joined me. We then went off to look for Mrs. Hardwood. She had come back in the shade of the Braak hedge.'

'Why did you all separate?' I said flippantly. 'Don't you realise that alibis are important?'

Mrs. Hardwood looked at me fixedly.

★ ★ ★

By one o'clock Mrs. Braak hadn't put in an appearance. I had been restive for the last hour. I knew that Combrink was feeling the strain too. This could be the end of the affair, the mysteries could be resolved, the guilty brought to bay, the unguilty given their precious freedom.

The minutes after one ticked by even more ponderously.

'She should be here,' he grumbled to me. 'I just hope she hasn't changed her mind. It could be dangerous for her. It could be dangerous for other people. She may of course still have her own double game to play, but I wish to God she'd come now.'

He looked down at his watch once again. I think several of the guests noticed that something was amiss. They were becoming curious, even nervous. We didn't want that to happen.

A quarter past one.

'I'm going to see her, even if it means upsetting her,' said Combrink. 'We can't go waiting indefinitely. I'm going to get the truth out of her at all costs, whether she wants to co-operate or not.'

He was forestalled by the sudden appearance of Mr. Braak, looking red-faced and anxious. I had only to see him for my own unreasonable fear to start up.

'I'm looking for my wife,' he announced to the assembled company. 'Have you seen her? I'm worried, man.'

He turned to the sergeant, who had quickly come to his feet.

'Sergeant, I'm worried, man, I haven't seen her since I went into the lands this morning. With this other thing happening on the farm, I don't like it. I know she can look after herself. But still I don't like it. If you haven't seen her, I must go on looking, but you must help me, please.'

He made as if to leave, but he was detained by Combrink.

'Just a second, Mr. Braak. You say you last saw her when you went out this morning. What time was that?'

'About nine-thirty, I think.'

'You didn't see her again?'

'I didn't see her — that's the funny part . . . '

'What do you mean?'

'I didn't see her, but I heard her all right. Just before twelve. I was coming back to the house, up the lands, when I heard her in the house.'

'Heard her?'

'Man, she was shouting at someone. Her voice was loud. She was angry.'

'The other person — who was that?'

'That's the strange part. The voice was too low for me.'

'Could you hear anything she said?'

'No, I couldn't. But her voice was loud, man. She was mad about something. I hurried up to the house then. When I got there she had disappeared. That was also strange. Her visitor wasn't to be seen, either. I went round the house calling for her — no answer. Just silence. It was queer.'

He mopped his liberally perspiring brow.

'I've been looking for her — just can't find her.'

'Where were your dogs?'

'Man, we can't keep any. She can't stand dogs. I know on the farm it's wrong, but we've never had trouble before. Now this. It's queer, man.'

'Something's wrong all right,' said Combrink. 'We'd better all spread out looking for her.'

He had second thoughts as he surveyed us.

'No, we won't do that. She couldn't have got far from the house. I think you come with me, Mr. Braak and Mr. Digby. If you don't mind, Miss du Mont, we'll take Tiger with us.'

We started off with Tiger on a leash, moving behind the dam towards the Valley of the Braaks. Along the hedge, through it, and towards the house. It wasn't a long search.

On the goblin-studded lawn Tiger whimpered and began to drag us back to the hedge. When Combrink let him off the lead he bounded ahead. Hurrying behind him we saw him sniffing at what seemed to be a bundle of clothes. It was Mrs. Braak, her neck turned up, her head thrown backwards.

The thin red line told us all we wanted to know.

★ ★ ★

Mr. Braak broke down completely. He fell on his knees beside her, weeping profusely and murmuring over and over again. 'My treasure, my treasure, my treasure — who has done this to you?'

I was deeply distressed by his manifestation of the affection that had existed between what I had regarded as two very hard-souled people. Combrink quite clearly was stunned by the latest calamity.

'This bastard has done it again, under our very noses! Fine protection I am! I should be murdered myself.'

'My treasure, who has done this to you?'

Thalia found us there. Her face was a mask.

'Again?'

'Again.'

'Keep the others away,' said Combrink. 'Please! For God's sake keep them away.'

Without a word Thalia went back to her homestead, crossing the lawns of her farm of blood.

We crouched beside the hedge waiting for Mr. Braak to recover a few of his wits.

'We'll take her up to the house,' said Combrink. 'This time I have to get across the water somehow, even if I have to swim for it. Yet,' he said, and hesitated, 'I can't leave you people alone, although, God knows, I haven't been much protection so far.'

Bitterness and disappointment were stamped on his face, on his dejected back, his large helpless hands.

'She behaved foolishly,' he said. 'She played with death. She knew the answer, and this person,' I noticed that he now avoided giving it a sex, 'knew that she knew. That was the end of her.'

He bent over the sobbing Mr. Braak.

'Come, Mr. Braak,' he said with his rough kindness. 'Help us take her up.'

The big man seemed beyond words as the three of us struggled up with our ugly burden, her legs insisting on dangling loose, or an arm, or a sudden ringletted curl. I hadn't realised before that she had curly hair. We took her through to the main bedroom of The Grapevine, placed her on the Braak's double bed. Combrink turned to Mr. Braak.

'You can't stay here tonight. You'll have to come back to Miss du Mont's with us.'

'I won't leave my wife. I won't leave my treasure.'

'You will have to share my rondawel with me, Mr. Braak.'

'Does that mean I'm under arrest?'

'Yes, you could call it a sort of an arrest, as much as I can arrest anyone here. I want to arrest you against the danger of being on your own. Besides,' he added, 'I'll have all my strange birds in one nest this time.'

12

The weather, I believe in retrospect, was one of the agencies that helped drive our visitor mad. This visitor was pinned down by the rain and floods; movement became tricky, dangerous; the sudden black skies seemed to encourage perversity. That afternoon it began raining again, the fierce drops steadily puncturing the air. It must have been even heavier than I thought because, looking out of my rondawel window, I saw the water slowly encroaching on the garden. The valley must have been saturated.

We had been confined to the house by the weather, and by the wish of Combrink. We had all chosen to keep to our rooms, the sergeant sharing his with Braak. We were now in the full madness of our ordeal; we didn't seem any longer to be part of that sane world beyond the water. We were all waiting to die, one by one, until only a single person was left.

Help from outside, we felt, would come too late.

I shook myself. One had to be roused from this perverse lethargy, because this was the sort of conduct that would benefit our unknown adversary. We had to keep our nerves, our wills, our mental processes, alive at all costs. But the world seemed bleak, a watery hell that reflected the hell of being in this house.

That afternoon we had nothing to do but wait. We were waiting for the storm to burst, for the fury to explode on us. I sat in my room most of the afternoon, watching the water creep up to the house. It was rising. Like a stealthy creature it had come up softly beyond the avenue. I could see the beginning of its channels on the lawn. My state of shock was now so profound that I could hardly feel the horror of the afternoon's discovery. I was more interested in the water, in its inexorable progress towards the house. We were shut in with a murderer — or perhaps not. Perhaps the fair-haired André, so long believed dead was outside. Or Bert Price.

I could hear the chatter of the weavers at the dam. Every now and again one would come looping over the Jacaranda trees, set in flight by his angry companions. They too had been known to murder in the fury of their greed.

Then I heard a bird voice I hadn't heard before on the farm, the ghostly voice of the coucal: 'Woo-woo-woo-woo.' The rain bird. That large black and white bodied, that chocolate winged, terror of the weak. A coward to men, seldom seen, he chose the nests of the unsuspecting, showed his claws, disappeared. 'Woo-woo-woo'. The sound continued dolefully over the roof top.

Outside my window the poinsettias with their large red petals were dripping what seemed to be drops of colourless blood. All feeling had been dehydrated; there seemed to be no colour now. Below them were the Christ thorn, small bursts of flame, with the thick spikes piercing out of the fleshy stems, like agony.

The rain continued, the water came closer.

Thalia brought in a tray of tea.

'I've sent, or taken trays to each of the rondawels,' she announced. 'No one, I imagine, feels much like company today. But I'm coming to have mine with you. I want to talk to you, Simon.'

Normally I would have welcomed Thalia. Today I wished she had taken her tea elsewhere. I tried to put a bright face on it. She was not deceived, however.

'You don't really want to talk to me, do you?'

She didn't wait for a reply, but went on immediately:

'Simon, you don't think I'm . . . that I'm responsible for all this, do you? That I wanted the President's gold, or the du Mont gold, or whatever you wish to call it; that I killed Judith because she had found out what I had wanted to know, and because of some trick of fate had always missed? You don't think I had the du Mont madness, do you?'

Even a day before I should have said firmly 'no'; perhaps even amusedly 'no'. I couldn't say that to Thalia today.

'I don't blame you,' she said. 'It hasn't been much of a holiday has it?'

225

Her smile was wry, infinitely sad. Thalia had always been proud of her home and its spirit. I suspected that she had had most to do with that spirit, not her dry-humoured, gold-obsessed father, or her drab mother.

'At present I don't want to deflect your suspicion if it does indeed rest on me, but I do want to say something else — while there's time.'

Her voice took on a new urgency.

'Simon, I believe that André is on this farm, now. I didn't want to believe it, but I've become obsessed with the notion. I've felt his presence in so many things, intangible — but I've felt it.

'Look at it another way. Someone outside this house must have done the killings, unless it was Braak himself. I begin to feel that less and less. Someone outside, because this morning everyone here was in sight of everyone else. Except . . . '

I saw that she had suddenly thought of it, the thought that had made me sick with misery, for I could not bear the notion of youth and beauty corrupting, destroying itself by evil.

'Except Tony,' she said.

'You're not quite right,' I replied. 'About the others. Look at it *this* way. Charmaine and I were together examining that wretched scrap-book, but we separated when I went for a swim. You were on the stoep then, but only for a moment.'

'She would have had to be very quick,' said Thalia.

'Aren't murderers who are obsessed with their need and their power reputed to be lightning quick in taking the opportunity?'

'I, too, was alone then.'

'Of course. So was I, unless Combrink from his window saw me swimming. Combrink, for that matter, was alone. You left your servants I guess several times to go into the house. They were alone, together if you like, but in the eyes of the suspecting, they could be seen to have a sinister resentment in common.'

'No one escapes,' she said.

'That's the teasing part: we try to keep them together, but everyone establishes what I would call an un-alibi. Take those who went down to the trees to draw. Samuel went later than the others. He joins Eric who in the meantime has separated from Mrs. Hardwood, who returns — along the Braak hedge.'

There was again one of those silences, which we tried to cover by drinking our tea. We were joined, quite undramatically, by Mrs. Hardwood herself.

'That's quite true,' she said. 'I did return along the Braak hedge.'

I had got over my first surprise.

'You saw nothing?'

'Have some tea,' said Thalia, interrupting me.

'No thank you — as you know, I've had my own tea in the confines of my rondawel. No, I saw nothing — but I think I heard, something . . . '

We were waiting for her to go on.

'Two voices. I didn't recognise them. They were both soft, breathless, husky. Then Mrs. Braak's voice a little above the other. It was strange what I think I heard.'

'Yes?'

'It doesn't make sense, but I think what

she said was: 'Again you have this fascination, again you use it.' Then they moved higher up, quickly, and I lost them.'

'Was this when I saw you coming along the hedge?'

'No, at least twenty minutes earlier. When I turned to join Eric and Samuel I must have been near where — where the body was, if it was there already. But I didn't see it.'

'Listen to the rain,' said Thalia. She seemed unable to concentrate. I looked at her curiously. She didn't turn from where she stood at the window.

'You know, there's something queer,' said Mrs. Hardwood suddenly. 'But it's unrelated to this case, I'm sure. I can't see a connection. And everyone's entitled to their secret.'

Thalia's back hardened. She said nothing.

'No, I'm not going to tell you. I would have liked, I know, to have kept my own secret. I wonder what you think of me now. Mine was a medical secret; this, in a sense, is one too. On second thoughts, I was wrong even to mention it.'

The rain was beating down much harder. Millions upon millions of gallons of water must have poured into the valley.

'The water's crossing the lawn,' said Thalia. 'Like some slow beast, crawling nearer, about to destroy us.'

I went to stand beside her at the window. It was quite true. I would have believed it impossible of this farm. Waves were spilling across the lawn, breaking softly against the wall of the rondawel. I could hear the soft lapping sound, quietly sinister.

'If this inundation continues, you know, we'll have to be evacuated. If there are any of us left. By the way, where did you put those books?'

I was not prepared for this sudden change of attack.

'Under the bed,' I said.

'I see.'

Mrs. Hardwood left us to go back to her own rondawel.

'Expecting another visitation tonight?' asked Thalia quietly.

'Surely this person wouldn't attempt it again?'

'I know the mind of this person. I know that when this person sees what is suspected to be a weak link, that link must be removed. I know that tenacity, that ruthlessness. Be on your guard, watch out for your life.'

We were silent again. Thalia managed a dry laugh.

'What a warning to give a guest bent on relaxation! Well, my sweet, I must love and leave you, to prepare the fortress against the floods without, and, if only I could, against the monster within.'

I was on my own, still looking at the water as it lapped beneath me. The rain bird had once more begun its call across the valley. As I watched, an owl darted from the avenue, swooped towards me, poised for a second in the air, dived down to the water, and came up bearing a field-mouse in its claws. The bird disappeared into the dark woods.

Perhaps I should have looked at my books again, but I had lost interest. Lethargically I was simply waiting for the next blow to fall.

★　★　★

By supper time I had roused myself, however. We were a silent, glum community as we sat round the table. Mr. Braak was also there this time. Thalia, with a sudden drop in taste, I thought, had produced a delicious red wine and insisted on each of us having some, almost in the manner of a celebration. I had very little. I was determined to keep awake at all costs.

When I went to my rondawel I decided to do more than keep awake. I must be prepared. To be caught, if only caught waiting, was to risk having my throat cut. I must try to prepare the element of surprise, not wait for it to come to me. If this weird bird chose to risk another visitation — the chances seemed slight, despite Thalia's warning — it would come soon. I must rest in the meantime, and also be seen to be going to bed. I undressed with the curtains open, inviting a Peeping Tom. I climbed into bed, drew the books from under it, piled them on the table next to me. The bait, too, must be clearly seen. I lay for an hour or more going through the books, finding nothing.

As soon as I switched off the light, I rolled out of bed leaving the pillows stretched out in simulation of my sleeping self. I dressed as quietly, as quickly as I could. Should I wait outside, and watch? Should I wait inside? Surely if he (or she) came again, the window stunt, twice abortive, would not be repeated? The door would be opened, even though I were to leave it locked. A cunning person would now have prepared himself for a direct assault. Yet, if I stayed in the room, I was exposing myself to danger. Foolishly I had brought no weapon with me. Yet surprise would be on my side. I gripped the torch tightly.

The rain had stopped. The eaves of the thatch were dripping softly; there were the smaller stirrings of the farm. A cock, incongruously, crowed at the night. This was followed by the responsive hooting of the wood owls. What I thought to be an hour passed; then another began. I thought I heard a door opening, but couldn't be certain.

I waited again. A quarter of an hour passed.

I was becoming cramped and sore standing against the wall. How I longed to be in bed!

Then I heard it. A soft rustling sound, like a rat crossing the stoep. A key was being turned in my door. The upper half opened. I saw the night sky. The air, violently fresh after the rain, poured in.

The lower half of the door opened. I was no longer alone in my room. Not so much a shadow, but a dark blot moved towards the bed. I was foolish to have exposed myself, but clung to my element of surprise — so I thought. I switched on the torch, and flashed it on the shadow in front of me.

I had not reckoned on the quick reaction of the thing. The torch was knocked from my hand, I fell against the wall, and slid quickly down, for the blade had come sweeping past where I had been a moment before. I tried to catch out, realised that as soon as I was found, my moments would be numbered. My flaying arm caught the leg of the table. In the flash a crisis allows, I realised that only noise would save my life. I gripped the leg as firmly as I could, and brought the loaded table crashing down on top of me.

At least, I thought, as I lost consciousness, this creature would not even be able to reach towards the books it sought.

13

When I came to they were bending over me: Combrink, Thalia, Eric, Samuel, Charmaine. Within a few moments Mrs. Hardwood joined us.

I grinned foolishly up at them.

'What the hell do you think you're doing?' asked Combrink, his face pallid with fright.

'Trying to get myself murdered,' I replied weakly. It was a poor joke, but quite courageous in the circumstances.

Combrink turned to the people watching.

'I think you had better get back to your rooms,' he said.

'There's nothing to worry about, as you can see.'

When we were alone, he spoke again.

'You know, it's strange. I kept watch, and nothing passed me. I had the dog with me and he didn't react. What sort of a thing is this?'

'Where were you watching?'

'On the lawn. I thought I could see the whole house then.'

'This person, I think, crossed the stoep.'

'He could've come from the outside rooms. Braak didn't appear after the crash. Neither did Dr. Thurle, for that matter. Perhaps they thought, or one of them, it would be best to seem as though they hadn't heard.'

'And of course you couldn't vouch for Braak because you were out on the lawn watching.'

'Whatever this thing is, it's got the silence and the speed of a panther.'

'I wonder whether we'll — have the speed to catch it?'

Combrink didn't reply. With a draining of courage, I saw the burly man had completely lost confidence in himself.

There was nothing further to do but go to bed.

I didn't sleep. But neither did I have a further visitation.

★ ★ ★

The sun, as before after these storms, was bright and fierce the following morning. The waters had receded to beyond the avenue, and had left small pieces of bric-à-brac and drowned rats and birds on the lawn. The humidity became unbearable.

We looked incongruously normal when we met for breakfast. Yes, we were all there. It was as though we realised this was to be a roll call for final assembly. I had no reason to feel this, but there was an air of conclusiveness about the gathering. Monica's apathy was nearing its end, and there was a restlessness in the girl that was disturbing. Mrs. Hardwood's mouth was set in a tight, straight line; she looked as if she were trying to fit an awkward piece into the nearly complete picture. Charmaine was alternately sulky and bright, in her usual manner. Fierce as her friendship for Mrs. Braak had been, her death had left her untouched.

We all seemed to have forgotten the body shut in its room at The Grapevine.

Even Mr. Braak was able to make conversation. The normal atmosphere was unreal, crazy. But I, too, felt that the party had settled down, felt that this dangerous hide-and-seek game was nearly over. I had no reason for this, and was still depressingly conscious of the bruises occasioned by the previous night's fall.

The paw-paws were good, the newly picked oranges brightly aromatic. I had, suddenly, a renewed lust for life, even while I was feeling my bruises. If only we could come to grips with our unknown opponent. It was not so much the danger any more that mattered, as our extreme ignorance of what it was we were fighting. We had been on the brink of knowledge several times, but a swift cunning had defeated us. Mrs. Braak had certainly had the answer, but her greed had contributed to her end. I had almost seen the beast, but darkness had intervened. Mrs. Hardwood was distinctly troubled by something she knew. There were so many touchings on a truth that seemed infinitely complicated, and they had all led to nothing. Was there, in fact, a link between them — between the murders and the gold, between that old du Mont story and the present disasters? I couldn't make the connection any longer: to me it all seemed madness.

After breakfast Combrink spoke to me. The man seemed utterly dejected, a sleep walker moving in darkness.

'You know, when you first brought this case to me, I was super-confident. I thought: 'I'll have the answer in a very short while, long before those smart-alecky detectives even begin to arrive.' Now I pray they'll come quickly. I thought I had some leads, but all the trails are false. What is he waiting for? Is he waiting for the floods to subside so that he can get off the farm, or . . . '

And here he put his finger on the truth.

' . . . or is he still waiting, crazily, to look for something, or finish something? These deaths were unimportant to him. I have a feeling that there are, in fact, other people that he would rather destroy.'

He stopped, and stood looking at the debris on the lawn, at the dead birds and the field mice.

'This has been a strange time,' he said. 'We've never had floods like these in the valley, and probably never will again. Was it all coincidence? Or did the storms bring out the madness? Or the madness come because he couldn't find what he was looking for, and because the flood waters made it even more difficult, made it impossible?'

After a pause he continued:

'These are the questions one asks. I think I should tell you something else because you'll be in charge in a sense this morning. While these people were out Miss du Mont and I searched the rooms, but found nothing that made sense, to us, anyway. It's all just been a lot of blanks.

'I want you to keep an eye on things this morning. I have to go back there . . . '

He indicated the direction of The Grapevine.

'I'll be going with Braak, and I think we'd better take the old girl with us as well.'

He was now looking at Mrs. Hardwood, where she sat blankly behind her spectacles.

'She's skilled at — at working with bodies. We'll need her.'

The three of them started off for The Grapevine quite soon after that. Thalia, as usual at this time of morning, went off to the kitchen. Charmaine and Samuel sat together on the settee on the stoep. Monica stayed on, watching them, watching Eric and Tony where they stood on the lawn inspecting the flood debris. Combrink had made it clear that no one was to leave the house.

The morning began quietly enough. It was to prove a momentous period, mounting on a ripple of incidents to its climax.

It began with Charmaine wanting to show her husband something she had come across in her scrap-book. He expressed mild interest and she went off to collect it. She was in her rondawel for several minutes, strangely quiet. Then we heard her opening and shutting things, opening and shutting them again, until she burst out of the room.

There were angry red blotches on her face as she confronted us.

'Where is it? One of you has got it. Some snoopy pest has taken my scrap-book. Where is it, damn you, all of you

— I'm sick of you all! Samuel, make them give me back my scrap-book!'

'Please dear, don't get excited. We'll find it. Where did you leave it?'

'You know where I left it. On the table.'

'Yes, I saw it there yesterday afternoon. Was it there last night — didn't you take it into the sitting-room?'

'I saw it there before I went to bed, I tell you! Why don't you believe me?'

She began shouting in a petulant, childish voice.

'Who's got it? Damn you!'

Thalia had heard the shouting and she came out.

'It must be somewhere,' she said, trying to quieten the girl.

'You're just like him! He said that too. This bloody place of yours! Even a scrap-book has got to be stolen here!'

To placate her I asked each in turn whether they had seen it. Monica as answer tossed her head angrily. Eric and Tony hadn't seen it.

Desmond was sent for, and he was asked the same question. His answer surprised us.

Yes, he had seen it.

Where was it?

He politely asked us to go with him. We trooped silently behind him into the kitchen where Samantha was standing at the scrubbed table peeling potatoes with a long wicked looking knife. She hardly seemed surprised at our appearance. There we were, all that remained of us at the Bloedplaas homestead, in the kitchen. Nine of us in all, as if at a secret ritual ceremony.

Desmond crossed elaborately to the coal stove, which Thalia insisted on having in the kitchen. (It was her opinion that no cooking was as good as that done over coal.) With the iron handle he lifted out the plate, and indicated the coals burning beneath. They were not very hot, but as I leaned over I could see what looked like sheets of ash. About half of the spine was intact. I fished it out with a pair of tongs. It was the remainder, certainly, of Charmaine's ill-fated scrapbook. She confirmed this in a quiet, crushed manner.

We looked at each other silently. What

could it have contained that it was so necessary to destroy it?

'It must have been stolen from the rondawel last night,' Charmaine said in her new, subdued voice. Our visitor, in fact, had had to collect two things: the scrap-book and my mysterious volume. He had succeeded in gaining possession of the one. The other still eluded him.

The coal fire was kept burning all night. The scrap-book could have been fed to the flames at any time before the servants came into the kitchen in the morning.

'I'm terribly sorry,' said Thalia.

'It doesn't matter,' Charmaine replied off-handedly.

We trooped back to the stoep, most of us going to our rooms. Charmaine and Samuel returned to the sofa. When I went to my room I heard them murmuring together.

I shouldn't perhaps have left them, but I wanted to look at my book again, for I was now filled with an overpowering sense of imminent revelation. The solution must be there, somewhere.

I spent the best part of an hour going through the notes of the book in which Judith had written 'p.57'. I read through a rather poor history of the Eastern Transvaal gold diggings; I examined ways of extracting gold, methods for detecting ore, and so on. I looked at statistics. I went back to the history. It seemed, in fact, one of the driest, the most uninformative, I had ever tried to plough through.

I must after all have been wrong and the whole hunt through the books nothing but a wild goose chase. There was clearly something else in the room that the mysterious visitor so desperately wanted, sufficient to make him call on me three times.

I looked around trying to think what it was. There was nothing promising that I could see.

Then from sheer enervation, I flipped back to page 57, and somewhat sightlessly began to look at the faces of those old diggers and the small printed names beneath.

It hit me full in the face.

I knew who our visitor, who the beast of the valley, was. The truth was clear to me immediately, though not the complications. I knew with an absolute certainty who had been responsible for our sufferings.

It was one of the names in fine print at the bottom of the plate that my eye had lighted on:

'Mr. Samuel Smith'.

14

His guilt was absolutely certain to me, why precisely I can't tell you. That certainly was the entry he had not wanted us to see, and we had touched on it multiple times. I could hear the low murmur of his voice and Charmaine's as they sat together on the couch.

As my mind edged further on, I could make out a little of it. The name had belonged to an old digger who had been in the area long before we had ever heard of it, in fact before we had ever been born. There were two possibilities: this man was a descendant of the old Samuel Smith, and he had taken a grave risk in retaining the name. That, or — the name was assumed, either for a purpose, or, probably, it was one of those unconscious choices from having seen the name before. A sub-conscious fixation on the part of the borrower. He realised, only after he had chosen the name, what had happened. To have the name was dangerous, because if the association was seen it became an arrow pointing direct at one person, one person only. The rumours of the ghosts, the tangled trail — all these became unimportant.

I puzzled backwards and forwards, but mostly over one thing. Why destroy the scrap-book? I could see now that it must have been easy enough to do so. But why? I had seen the mining articles. There had been nothing there that I thought could have pointed to him. But Mrs. Braak had also seen the scrap-book, and she had stumbled on the truth by that route. The whole truth was still hidden, and I had to find it before we could make a move and — pray God — before he could act again.

The hardest task of all now confronted me. I had to pretend that nothing had been discovered. I had to let him go on thinking himself unsuspected. Yet — and here I shivered again: he had found out easily enough about the others — Judith and Mrs. Braak — when they had acquired the fatal knowledge. My life could now be the penalty. As I thought these thoughts a shadow crossed the half open door.

I was on my feet immediately, and moved to the opening, straining to appear casual, my knees quaking beneath me. Samuel and his wife were still on the couch. I saw Eric had moved past my door on his way to the stoep. Tony was still on the lawn.

I came out, forcing myself to make brightish conversation. To myself I appeared horribly stilted. Eric had begun a drawing. Charmaine had recovered her good humour, and was chattering animatedly. For the moment Samuel Smith was sitting silently beside her, looking quietly at myself and at Eric. I didn't like his vague eyes resting on me like that.

Monica then appeared on the stoep. She sat down, watching us all.

As I made desultory conversation my mind was whirling. Right, I had found out who it was. But how was I to move towards the complete truth? How could I fit the next piece into the jig-saw with which I had been saddled? How could I show that all roads led to, all fingers pointed at — Samuel Smith?

Then I perceived the next move, and knew that I would have to play it carefully, on my own for the moment. I couldn't tell Combrink just yet, or Thalia. My next approach would have to be Mrs. Hardwood.

Though the sun was a brilliant coin in a glittering blue sky, I heard the ghost again. 'Woo-woo-woo-woo' sounded through the valley. Charmaine shuddered.

'That thing gives me the creeps. What is it?'

'A rain bird,' I told her.

'A rain bird with the sun out as bright as that! You love a joke, don't you? If we have more rain I'll go mad, honestly. Samuel and I must get off this hideous farm as soon as we can. Mustn't we, Samuel?'

'Yes,' he agreed, his mild eyes poised on my face like a touch.

'I wonder where those other people are,' Charmaine continued, looking hastily over her shoulder. 'They shouldn't leave us too long alone — although I suppose there's no doubt now that that man Braak is the murderer? He was in my scrap-book, you know. Don't think I missed

251

that. What do you think they're doing all the time?'

'Preparing the body,' said Monica.

Charmaine looked at her with repugnance.

'You give me the creeps, too. I wouldn't be surprised if you had a hand in it. You're the one with the surgical skill, aren't you? A nice neat cut, wasn't it?'

'Charmaine! Charmaine!' protested her husband.

Desperately trying to change the conversation, I turned to Eric.

'What are you drawing?'

'A very interesting face,' he said between gritted teeth.

I went across to him. He made no attempt to cover the drawing. This was a dangerous game, cat and mouse, the cat watching. It was of Samuel Smith without his glasses, the eyes peering out with a look I seemed to recognise. I think my finger was about to touch the heart of the mystery, but I had to be sure.

I tried to make our conversation as commonplace as I could.

'On what do you base your perception?' I asked.

'On an artist's instinct,' he answered.

Samuel Smith was watching us mildly.

Thalia then came out with tea. Samuel rose to help her, coming past where Eric had sat drawing. But the sketch had already been covered, and Eric held the block firmly in his hand. It is just possible that by doing that he saved his life.

The tea-party was to me a macabre affair. Conventional on the surface, but with all manner of currents beneath.

I could see that Thalia was puzzled by something, that she was feeling her way through a shadowy world towards truth. What could it be that she had got hold of? Or was I, now hyper-sensitive, perceiving signs that simply weren't there?

The bird of the valley had begun his 'woo-woo-woo-woo', but now, as if declaring his defeat, his voice was overlaid by the sharp excited chatter of the weavers, the 'coo-coo-roo-coo-coo' of the turtle dove, by the sparrows that descended onto the bric-à-brac lawn and were hopping from spoil to spoil, chattering and quarrelling. Then there was the wagtail, stepping daintily along, his white bottom bobbing beneath the springy tail.

'Their world is returning to normal,' said Thalia. 'I have an idea that our own bad season is almost over.'

'Aren't you being optimistic?'

This was Charmaine's comment.

We heard the others returning along the Braak hedge. As they came onto the lawn I went out to meet them, as casually as possible. Braak's face was the ugly ashen colour I had seen before — I could guess that this encounter with his wife had not been pleasant. Mrs. Hardwood was bland behind her spectacles. Combrink, so robust at one time, seemed to have become merely a burly, negative shadow. It would be wrong to speak to him until I was sure. And what did one do then? Undertake an arrest? So far there was this one sure thing; the rest were guesses. The final pieces of the jig-saw would still have to be fitted into their places.

'Mrs. Hardwood,' I said, keeping my voice steady, and, I hope, light, 'there's a curiously shaped Kaffirboom just beyond the lawn near the avenue I'd like you to see. That's if you haven't seen it already.'

They stopped in their tracks. It was inordinately queer to greet a funeral party with this sort of information. I immediately realised my blunder, and tried to cover up.

'I know it's an odd time,' I explained clumsily. 'But the storm, by ripping down branches, showed it to me only this morning.'

'I'll have a look,' she said.

As we drew near to the tree (I had chosen a genuine tree because I knew this might be checked on later — I had not been quite that foolish) — as we got near, she said to me casually:

'That was mismanaged.'

'I know. But I had to talk to you, now — the more people who can work towards the truth, the better insurance of safety we have.'

'Why choose me as, I presume, your first confidant?'

Her eyes glittered behind her glasses.

'Because you have noticed something odd, and . . . ' I meant this second part: 'because I trust you; it may, on this occasion, be with my life.'

This was somewhat melodramatic, but I could see her face beginning to glow with pleasure. To be trusted once again!

'I want to suggest the name of the person you had some reservations about, who had a personal secret which you felt should be respected.'

'I may still feel that that secret deserves respect, Mr. Digby. Although dismissed as a professional nurse, I still am possessed by the ethics of my calling.'

'You must decide that for yourself, Mrs. Hardwood; but your answer may decide life or death.'

'Go on.'

'It's Samuel Smith, isn't it?'

She was startled, but she said straightly enough:

'You're right.'

'Now, I suppose, I have to convince you of the most difficult thing of all. That it's vital that you should tell me what you know about him.'

'It may not be difficult,' she said. 'Because, you see, I for my part trust *you*. I've read your books. I think I know the sort of person with whom I'm dealing.' She was almost apologetic now. 'I would of course like to know a little more first. It seems right, somehow.'

'To begin with, I think his name is assumed, that he's not the person he pretends to be.'

I could see that my information had struck home.

'That accords with what I know,' she said. 'Go on.'

'But who he is, no one knows — not here, anyway. He's quite clearly never been seen in this valley.'

'That may not be the case, you know. He may have been seen, often.'

'What do you mean?'

'First answer this. Do you suspect him of these murders?'

'I *know* he's the man we want. I can't at present show you proof that's conclusive, but I'm sure that I've hit on the secret.'

'All right, I trust you,' she said. 'The fact is this . . . '

Instinctively we turned to see that we were alone. Samuel and his wife were still on the couch. Eric and Tony, Combrink and Braak had their heads together in discussion.

'The fact is, that he isn't what he seems. I had better make myself clearer: that face is not the face he's had all his life. In other words, he is the product — the highly successful product, I'd say — of extensive plastic surgery.'

The ghost of the valley had stopped his calling just as the pieces came into place.

'Does that make sense in terms of your theories?' she asked.

'It makes sense of everything.'

'I've seen this sort of operation quite often,' she explained. 'My experience as a theatre sister was wide. He usually keeps his face safely in the shade, but on the few occasions I caught him in the sunlight, I saw signs that I recognised. I won't explain these now. I've been watching him steadily ever since, and became more and more sure. But I felt, because I had suffered myself, that if he hadn't spoken of it, or his wife, there was a good reason: I felt strongly, with a fervent sense of medical etiquette, that his privacy should be respected. I'm as sure of this operation as you are of his guilt. Nevertheless it would be best, I think, to have a second opinion before any action is taken.'

'Whom could we consult?'

'You have a competent surgeon here in Monica Thurle. I'm surprised she hasn't noticed it herself. But then a nurse often sees what a doctor leaves unobserved, especially when he or she is absorbed in other things.'

'I, too, would like another view of my theories before we proceed. I must talk to someone else.'

'To the policeman?'

'No, to someone before him — Thalia.'

'Yes, that seems right. But we'd better go in to lunch now if we don't want suspicions aroused. We must behave normally, I suppose.'

There was no doubt that Mrs. Hardwood would do her duty.

★ ★ ★

Lunch was another of the macabre affairs we had grown to expect at Bloedplaas.

Thalia was conducting most of the conversation. Combrink, Braak, Tony, Monica, Samuel Smith had become silent, or monosyllabic in their replies. An emotional storm was brewing. I hoped we would be in time to prevent its bursting on us.

Charmaine had started telling Mrs. Hardwood about her miserable scrap-book.

'I wonder who could have gone and burnt it. I'd like to get my hands on the wretch. It's like so many mean things that have gone on here.'

She clearly equated the destruction of her scrap-book with murder.

'It's a good thing,' she continued, 'that I took some of the photographs out, those you had written the captions for, Samuel?'

'What did you say?'

It was the sharpest question he had ever asked her in our presence. I could see his eyes glittering behind his glasses. His last resistance, just possibly, was giving. Charmaine, too, suddenly looked frightened.

'Why did you do that, dear?'

His voice had again become mild, but to me there seemed to be even more menace in it.

'Mrs. Braak asked for one or two. They didn't seem very important to me, the ones she wanted. And then she — died. I didn't have a chance of giving them to her.'

The conversation stumbled on. Perhaps the others hadn't noticed anything, although Thalia, I thought, had become increasingly restless as lunch proceeded. She found it an increasing strain to keep up her façade.

After lunch when the others had gone to their rondawels I had a chance to talk to her alone. I had decided, once more, on a direct attack.

'What is it that worries you about Samuel Smith, Thalia?'

She seemed relieved to be able to tell someone else what she had on her mind.

'I've been feeling it for days, and it hit me particularly during lunch. Although so unlike in looks and manner — I suppose it's my imagination — he reminds me of my brother.'

'He is your brother.'

'What did you say?'

'Thalia,' I said urgently, 'we have so little time left. That man Smith is the product of plastic surgery. Mrs. Hardwood spotted this. The name isn't his own. I found that name among the list of miners on the page Judith had marked. He must have picked it up from there.'

She spoke slowly, now filled with the dread of her life.

'I told you, didn't I, that André was unimaginative in certain directions. He could be cunning, but not imaginative. To invent a name, for example. He subconsciously remembered a name he'd seen. Then, too late, he knew he'd made a slip. Is that why Judith died?'

'Yes, I'm sure it is. At some stage, by some token, the girl gave herself away. If you remember her letter, Judith herself felt this. Because of what she knew she had to be silenced.'

'But why Mrs. Braak?'

Even that piece had fallen into place.

'He'd hated her for a long time, I think, and the Braaks were trying to get hold of the gold he coveted. There's a long story behind that death, I warrant you.'

'But there was also a more immediate cause. You remember the evening we were looking at the notes and letters. We had your father's note about the Pilgrim's Rest treasure. There was the note in block letters I had brought back with me. There was also Judith's letter. And there was the letter from your brother.

'Just then Mrs. Braak arrived with Charmaine. Charmaine had spent practically all day showing her that wretched scrap-book. There were, I know, numerous photographs and letters in it. Letters from her husband, probably. Certainly there were photographs with the captions written out by him. Why he let her bring the scrap-book I can't tell you. It's possible he just didn't know she had it with her. Perhaps he had even forgotten about it. By one of those quirks of destiny the revealing scrap-book arrives with the murderer.

'Mrs. Braak, as I say, had been seeing his handwriting all day. She comes here, sees the letter, and sees the similarity. No, similarity's not the right word — they were identical. She questions us about the handwriting, and in a flash hits on the truth.'

'But why question us about the other letters?'

'Ah, that was her cunning, her way of disguising the discovery she had made. For she suddenly sees a way to the gold she had thought about for so long. She keeps her knowledge to herself, and in so doing she spells out her doom.'

Thalia was trembling.

'I know my family was eccentric! I know he was bad — but this! Oh, the horror of it!'

I felt sorry for her as she sat there trembling silently, her golden farm plunged into the blackness of the shadow that hung over her life.

'What are we to do now?' she asked.

'The first thing is, to have the medical evidence confirmed.'

'Who would be able to do that?'

'Monica. Can she be trusted, do you think?'

'I'd trust her with my life.'

'We'd better get Mrs. Hardwood here, and Monica. We'll leave Combrink out of it for the moment — if we're seen together, there may be suspicions aroused. We are probably being watched all the time.'

'That girl in there with him, do you think she knows.'

'I'd be prepared to say she doesn't, that she met him after this operation. That her news about the snapshots was innocent and caught him, at last, off his guard.'

'Do you think he's beginning to crack?'

'I'm certain he is. This weather has driven him literally mad. For two reasons: one, because I think temperamentally he is unbalanced. A man who'll kill to cover up a name is simply not sane. Secondly, because I think the water is keeping him from what he wants. It's covering up his treasure ground.'

'Do you think the gold's here then?'

'Yes, I think your father brought it to the farm. It all fits in. I see something else, too, which I'm afraid I must tell you because it makes sense to me. There was this quarrel with the man David, Desmond's brother. He knew too much.

Your brother removes this obstacle, his nerve fails him (he was much younger then, remember), and he has to flee the farm. Meanwhile he knows your father has brought the gold to Bloedplaas. He disappears for a year or two. Then one day your parents receive news of him. You are sent away. Your brother re-appears. Desmond hears voices as Braak heard voices yesterday.

'The next day you come back. They have to see him again, and the pretext this time is a visit to a neighbour. They have, I suspect, a passenger they must get away from the farm. That passenger, however, has decided that the gold must be his, his alone. He'll come back for it, and by that time your father must be out of the way — and also your poor mother, simply because she knew the truth.

'On the bridge the car swerves, is made to swerve. Someone dexterously escapes because he is prepared. Your father and mother are sent to their deaths.'

'No, Simon! Not that!'

'At last after waiting and planning and brooding, after a time in which he makes a new life, acquires a new face and a new identity, your brother returns. He knows of the existence of your father's notes, but someone has beaten him to it — Judith. Judith also finds out something else, gives herself away. Their last meeting almost certainly reveals the sources of her information to him. For her knowledge she must pay the price. He removes your father's notes from her handbag. Later he comes to suspect that I now have the book that contains the clue to his identity. The hunt must continue.'

'Oh, Simon, it's all such horror, horror, horror!' she exclaimed, unconsciously echoing Macduff after he had stumbled on the murdered Duncan. For a moment she covered her face with her hands, trying to shut out this vision of her world.

'These were his battlements. This would be the source of his power. Our guests, particularly Judith, made their fatal entrance.'

'But, tell me, where do you think my father's notes are now?'

Her eyes glittered for a moment. I could see her fighting off the old, terrible du Mont interest.

'I think, almost certainly, they have been destroyed. He saw what was in them, memorised them, didn't want another Judith on the scene.'

'So, if he doesn't speak, the secret goes with him?'

'That's about it.'

Thalia sighed.

'Perhaps a good thing, too. The President's gold has caused far too much suffering.'

I slightly changed the subject.

'Let's do our little medical reconnaissance. We must be prepared, before night falls.'

Mrs. Hardwood and Monica were summoned. Mrs. Hardwood told her story. For the first time since Judith's death I could see Monica coming to life. Under her surface calm, she was vengeance personified.

'It's possible,' she remarked with too brittle a casualness. 'I'll watch him during tea, and let you have the verdict after that.'

She looked then at Mrs. Hardwood. I

could see yet a further growth in the respect she felt for her.

'I'm frightened,' Thalia said.

'I'm not,' Monica answered briskly.

Our afternoon tea party was, if possible, even more macabre, Monica studying Samuel Smith, his facial contours, the lines of skin drawn over the bones. Samuel, evidently, had been having some little difficulty with Charmaine. She turned to him, to his acute embarrassment, and aroused an anger that could, I thought, not be quelled for much longer.

'I'm not going to give you those snapshots, Samuel. I don't see why you should want to keep them for me. I'd like to show them to — '

She picked on me.

'Simon here. He may be able to include them in his latest book.'

After tea the four companions joined together again in the sitting-room.

'Mrs. Hardwood's right,' said Monica. 'He has, I think, had a great deal of plastic surgery. I don't know why I hadn't seen it before. I haven't been looking properly for days, of course. And . . . ever since I've come here I've had my eye on Tony. I watched him with Judith. I thought he was the person. I was wrong.'

She was bitter at her own blind folly.

'What do we do now?' asked Thalia. 'Do we tell Sergeant Combrink?'

'I don't quite know what to do,' I said. 'We may spill the beans too early; our case isn't cast-iron yet. Tomorrow, certainly, the roads will be passable — but, then again, tomorrow may be . . . too late.'

'I don't think we should tell him,' said Monica decisively. 'Those snapshots are producing what I would call a crisis.'

'But in the meantime,' said Mrs. Hardwood, 'that young woman is exposed to the most terrible danger.'

'Let me think about it,' I said, still indecisive.

But as evening drew in I had not yet fixed on the next move.

15

The paradise flycatcher was still on its nest when I went to look at it that evening. I could see its long cinnamon tail trailing out of the small bowl-like structure. Unbelievably, it had escaped the storm. It belonged to the farm, would stay on and allow its kind to multiply. Tiger, beside me, blinked eagerly, his tail wagging, wondering what this new interest was, wondering whether, now that the storms had subsided, we would once more continue our walks.

I couldn't make up my mind what to do, and I was sickened by my indecision. Should I tell the sergeant? I had come to believe that he was an incompetent, that he would spoil the whole thing by a rough, unwise move. Were we in a position to corner a beast at bay? That knife had been so efficient before.

Should we wait for night to fall? He certainly wouldn't move, wouldn't strike, before then. But I was wrong. I had Tiger to thank for averting a further tragedy.

When I came back to the homestead from the paradise flycatcher everyone was in the sitting-room, quiet over their drinks.

'Tomorrow we move,' said the sergeant. 'Tomorrow will make or break me.'

They were clumsy words, and for some reason they were deeply unpleasant in the closing evening haze.

Charmaine chose this particular evening to insist that her long-bullied husband should dress for dinner. She hadn't asked it of him before, but on this occasion she insisted on his dressing up.

He protested mildly. She insisted. He refused. She was unyielding, pettily obstinate as only she could be. Then he followed her, outwardly patient, but I knew — with a horrible sickening — that something had at last given in the man. Thalia, Monica, Mrs. Hardwood watched them vigilantly, each one, I felt, armed in her own particular way.

We might, as I suggested, have been too late had Tiger not given the alarm.

The hair stood out on his back, he bristled, began growling. We were all alert. The dog seemed to think for a moment, then bounded up and out to the Smith rondawel. He quivered before it.

I was behind him and threw myself at the door. It had been locked. I knew, too, that the windows would be sealed and the curtains drawn. But Thalia had been armed. She had a key and the door sprang open, revealing the scene inside.

Samuel Smith had lost his proficiency. He was like a man possessed, trying to get Charmaine down on the bed, to get her throat in the best position for cutting it.

'I'll get you, you bitch! I've suffered for eight miserable years! And today you have to tell them about those pictures! I'll get you!'

The girl was able to say nothing in her defence, silent in her terror, trying to squirm away from the blade he held, thrashing helplessly out with one arm.

This took a split second. Tiger was on him. He diverted what would almost certainly have been the fatal blow. Samuel's attention was turned and he slashed quickly at the dog, drawing blood. Tiger was silenced.

But Monica also was in the room. She, too, had armed herself. I saw her face set like that of an ancient fury, before her arm flashed down, something in her hand. She plunged it into Samuel Smith.

He seemed to stagger away, have a quick convulsion, and then, in turn, fall silent.

★   ★   ★

Charmaine was now whimpering on the bed. Tiger lifted his head. He had been badly cut. The figure of Samuel Smith lay inert, uncannily quiet now that his fury had been spent.

'Have you killed him?' asked Thalia.

'Don't be a fool,' said Monica. 'That's perhaps the quickest-acting drug I know. I'm glad I had it with me. He'll come round all right; he'll face what's coming to him.'

She had been revenged. In her own medical manner, she had spoken for Judith.

I told you that Mrs. Hardwood had been armed too. She had armed herself with her preparedness and mercy. Charmaine was given a sedative and comforted by the remarkable woman. That night Mrs. Hardwood took the girl to her room and eased her into sleep.

Samuel was kept under watch in his own rondawel. He took some time to come round. When he did so, near midnight I think, the words he murmured were surprising.

'The bridge!'

Thalia, Combrink and I were keeping watch. Those words meant something to Thalia, as they did to me. Perhaps she, too, had thought of the story of her parents' end. It must be something connected with that.

Samuel fell silent immediately.

Then, when I thought about his words, I wondered.

A little later he opened his eyes, smiled at his sister. The past and present had for the moment faded away; they were again children together. Thalia tried, gently, to comfort her brother.

★ ★ ★

There's not much more to tell, although we had by no means reached the end of tragedy. Thalia had hers. So did Charmaine. So did Braak. So did Monica. So, perhaps, did Samuel Smith. But that wasn't the end of it, even then.

The roads were still impassable the next day. But a launch arrived, and two policemen came up to the homestead. They were duly amazed at the havoc that had been wrought during our period — to coin an irony — of inactivity.

Their moves were clear, however. Mrs. Braak's body had to be taken across the water. Before that Samuel would have to go. He was handcuffed to Combrink, who did not intend letting the beast slip away from him this time. The sergeant would cling to the end to his charge.

Samuel had nothing to say to any of us before he left, except Thalia.

He had refused steadfastly to reveal what he knew about the treasure.

He glanced at his sister as he was about to be taken off.

'Forget about the gold,' he advised her, and attempted a smile that crinkled the plastic masterpiece of his face. 'It won't do you any good.'

What happened after that, we had to gather from the reports.

The two young policemen were in front, Combrink behind, handcuffed to his prisoner. They were crossing the deepest part of the flood waters when André, with one of those powerful animal movements of which he was so suddenly capable, threw himself out of the launch, pulling Combrink violently with him. The launch had shot on as if catapulted. It tried to turn in its tracks. The handcuffed men came up, the one struggling to survive, the other struggling for destruction. The stronger won. They disappeared under a cluster of reeds. When they were found half an hour later, the story had been told.

Thalia had been spared a drawn out court case, in which she would have seen her brother suffer, her family name hauled up for ugly public viewing. Combrink had been gallantly inefficient to the end.

★ ★ ★

That really is, I suppose, the end of the story. Except about the President's treasure.

That muttered phrase 'The bridge!' continued to bemuse me. When Mrs. Hardwood left the farm, with Charmaine in her care, when Eric and Tony left, when Monica left, I was alone with Thalia, and touched on the matter of 'The bridge' again.

Perhaps I'd better tell you about Monica first. Her face was almost cheerful when the time for leaving came. For some reason Thalia had absented herself. I was seeing her off on my own.

'You showed courage that night,' I remarked to her.

'Not as much courage as I'll show if I'm able to show you something else,' she replied.

She drove off down the avenue, under the eaves of the wood owls, leaving a small cloud of dust behind her, and also a puzzled Simon Digby.

'We're going to have a good look under

that bridge,' I said to Thalia later in the morning.

I saw to it that the search was properly, legally arranged. There were several diggers, and I joined in myself. We spent three days uncovering the mud, trying to spade as deeply into the most promising spots we could find. After the third day it was suggested that the search be abandoned. I pleaded for one more day.

On the fourth day, under the bridge where Thalia's parents had been sent to their deaths, we discovered the treasure in a neat tin trunk. The drying, clinging mud tried to hold it back, but we brought it to the light of day, on the spot where Thomas du Mont had buried it a decade before.

There weren't millions, I must tell you that straight away. But there was something approaching two hundred thousand rands in present-day currency. It was not minted gold, and there was nothing to show that it was the President's millions or part of it. Just a mysterious treasure that legend had spoken of and that Thomas du Mont had found and brought to his farm. With it he had also brought unceasing tragedy.

By the legal complications of an old digger's grant, Thalia through her father could claim a large proportion of the treasure, and she became a wealthy woman. Her money didn't go to charity. That would be an easy end to the story. It went to the valley she loved despite all the horror it had brought her.

★ ★ ★

Mr. Braak gave up The Grapevine, and moved south. He was not at all resentful about selling to Thalia, who removed the goblins and the toadstools, and turned the house into what she called her 'Winter Residence'. Her own home became the 'Summer Palace'. Both homes were used for guests. I learnt a little while later that Mrs. Hardwood had come to join her in her venture.

Mrs. Hardwood had looked after Charmaine for several months, but after that the girl recovered with amazing rapidity, and remarried. Thalia, with the older woman beside her, renamed the valley 'Boomvallei'. Valley of Trees. The Farm of Blood had disappeared into limbo.

It's amazing how quickly one recovers from an experience such as this. The farm was its old beautiful self when Monica and I visited it a year later. We had married a few months before that.

Thalia came out to welcome us, as of old.

'Hail, my dearest, truly dearest spirits.'

And, as before, we settled down for tea on the stoep. There was, apparently, a colony of visitors at the Winter Residence, but she seemed to have no one at the Palace.

'Where's Mrs. Hardwood?' I asked. 'Is she below in the Valley of the Braaks?'

'No, she's not at the Winter Residence. You'll see her quite soon.'

Monica wanted to rest. She thought it might be a good idea if Thalia and I, as old friends, had a chat together.

'Come with me,' said Thalia.

We walked out under the Jacaranda trees.

'The flycatcher was delivered of its young soon after you left,' she told me.

The weavers, as usual, were busy at their nest-making; a green dove had settled in one of the darkest trees.

Elsie had hysterics when she saw us setting off on a walk that would take us beyond the lawn. Tiger padded silently beside us.

We climbed up along the stream where I had gone so many times before. The tinkling water was at peace again.

'Now observe,' said Thalia, as we neared the pool where Tony and Judith had bathed that morning of the first terrible storm.

We looked through the foliage to where the pool lay sheeny in the sunlight. A young naked god was standing on the edge of the water, like Narcissus bent over his image, his bowed head slightly in shadow. His hands were poised quietly on sun-golden hips. Tony, as before — the transitory, eternal image of human beauty.

In the shade above the pool Eric and Mrs. Hardwood sat quietly, drawing.